# MY SORF
# MI LIBERTAD.

**ROBIN HARWICK**

Harwick, Robin.
*My sorrow. Mi libertad.*

First edition KDP
Morelia, Michoacán, México. June 2021.

ISBN 979-8-5208-4511-9

© Robin Harwick, 2021
  drrobin@robinharwick.com
  robinharwick.com

Editorial services and digital typesetting
  Qvixote Press
  leo@qvixote.press

Cover design
  Marciana Romero

Cover illustration
  Brittaney Drake

"The days went by sluggishly when I lived on the streets. The sun didn't come up until almost eight and went down by a little after four. That gave me an excuse to tuck myself into a sleeping bag for many hours of the day. We also spent several hours a day begging for money on the Ave. Between all of us, we managed to get enough money for one pay as you go cell phone. We took turns checking our messages on that phone – trying to stay connected to anyone we could think of. It felt like if I didn't have a phone, I'd be forgotten."

*For youth and families
impacted by the foster care system
and substance use disorders*

# About this book

The reasons for a child or youth's placement into foster care are numerous, complex, and often provoke controversy. Regardless of *why* children enter care and *if* we agree with those placement decisions – on any given day over 430,000 children and youth are in the foster care system in the United States. Nearly half of those children have a disability diagnosis, and children and youth of color are disproportionally represented in the foster care system. The long-term impact of these placements cannot be overstated. U.S. youth who transition directly from foster care to adulthood often endure underemployment, low educational attainment, homelessness, involvement with the justice system, and mental health issues. Most people agree the system is flawed and that children and youth suffer within it.

However, the side that is not often told is that youth in foster care are resilient, strong-advocates for themselves and others, and can beat the odds and achieve their dreams. *My sorrow. Mi libertad.*, is a story of strength, determination, and hope. Although a work of fiction, the characters are based on youth who experienced foster care, their families, and injection drug users who shared their life histories with the author during her academic research and professional career. Many of the people who participated in her research said they did so with the goal of "giving back." They frequently asked her to please share their stories to "help others."

This book is one way of Dr. Harwick fulfilling her promise to the people who shared their stories with her. May Didi's story brings hope to youth within the system and understanding to social workers, foster and adoptive parents, mental health professionals, lawyers, and other people who work with youth impacted by the foster care system.

MY SORROW.
MI LIBERTAD.

# I

# UPHEAVAL

I FORCED MY eyes open. It must've been a horrible dream. It couldn't be real. I slowly looked around the barren white room. My fears were confirmed. I was a ward of the state. My freedom was gone. There was a small three drawer white dresser between my bed and the next victim's bed, which was currently empty. There was nothing on the wall except a few small holes where someone once placed mementos of their past. In a panic I looked for my stuff. A large black trash bag and my backpack were in the corner of the room. The bag contained everything I could grab when CPS arrived. Honestly, I didn't even know where the rest of my stuff was. My mom and I moved frequently over the last couple years, and each time we left a little behind.

"Delores, time to get up. We have a busy day ahead." My door flew open, and the house mom burst into my room. "What do you want for breakfast?"

"Death," I replied as I covered my tear-stained face with the blankets.

"Come on, let's make the best of this. I'll see you in the kitchen in fifteen minutes. I put a clean towel in the bathroom for you, if you'd like to take a shower?"

How the hell was she able to act like it was a normal day? I could barely remember the previous day or how I ended up there. I think the caseworker dropped me off about 1am. By that time, I had spent so many hours cycling between anger and crying hysterically that I fell asleep almost immediately when my head hit the bed. I didn't even remember the nauseatingly nice lady's name. All I knew was that I needed to get out of there.

I needed to find my mom. Together we would figure a way out of the situation. We were always a team and no matter how shitty things got we figured it out. I knew my mom was going through some really hard stuff. She just needed some time. That's how I ended up couch surfing. I planned to give her a couple of months to straighten things out and then we would find a place to stay.

Don't panic, you can do this. C'mon Didi hold it together. Don't let them see you cry, I chided myself. I couldn't help it though. I was furious at that lady that came and stole me from my friend's house.

"I don't want to go," I screamed.

"I'm sorry, but you really don't have a choice. It's our job to make sure you're safe."

"Please. Please, don't make me go. My friends look out for me. I'm ok. I can handle this. I'm almost an adult anyway. I can take care of myself."

"You're only fifteen. You still need someone to take care of you. Our job is to make sure that is happening." *¡Con una chingada!* Why now? – I thought. The sound of the house mom's voice pulled me out of my head and back into the room.

"Delores, are you coming down? I made waffles."

Her voice was making my stomach turn. It was dripping with more sweetness than the Organic Grade A syrup she would probably pour on the homemade waffles. I heard giggling. Oh no, who else is here? Did I need to talk to other people beside that lady? The thought was horrifying.

"I don't wanna come out," I yelled. A moment of silence followed.

"Delores, we need to go meet with the caseworker. Don't you want to eat first?"

Food was the last thing on my mind. A hot shower did sound good though, it had been a few days since I had one. My mom hadn't had time to cut my hair in a bit, so it was really long. My hair was thick and wavy and could get big and out of control easily. In my exhaustion, I forgot to tie it up before bed. I needed to tame it a bit before facing the world. I also had puffy racoon eyes from the long night of crying. My eyeliner wasn't waterproof enough to withstand the flash flood generated by this situation. I extracted myself from the bed and grabbed the garbage bag with my clothes. I always do my best thinking while in a long hot shower – maybe I would find answers in there. The perky lady was still asking questions; I didn't answer.

The bathroom was senselessly big, and everything was shiny and spotless. All the towels had matching hand towels and washcloths. There were four sets, all different colors. There were two sinks on the long marble counter. A set of thick pink towels were folded up perfectly between the sinks. I guessed those were me. I turned on the shower, and the water was hot almost immediately. It was one of those fancy spray nozzles that you can change from feeling like a misty rain to where it hurts when it hits your skin. I had to stretch to reach the shower head. I set the spray to hit me as hard as possible. Maybe it would wash away the nightmare? Attached to the wall was a dispenser labeled shampoo, conditioner, and body wash. They all smelled like roses. I don't know exactly when the sobbing began or how long I sat on the floor of the shower. The tears wouldn't stop. My fingers became prunes. I was startled back to my current reality with the sound of pounding on the door.

"Delores, answer me. If you don't answer me right now, I have to come in. You're scaring me. Are you ok?"

I found the strength to squeeze out the words, "I'm ok."

"Please come out." She begged sounding more scared than perky now.

"Ok."

"Thank you," she responded gently.

I dried myself off and fished around in my bag for something to put on. Not too much to choose from so I slipped on a pair of jeans, an old Soundgarden shirt of my mom's, a plain black hoodie that was way too big for me, and my black rubber rose-covered boots. I have no idea whose hoodie it was. I wiped clear a small circle of steam from the mirror. I kind of didn't want to see myself. My mascara and eyeliner still stained my cheeks, even after all that time in the shower. I scrubbed furiously. The tears gushed again. I looked paler than I should have, even for that time of year. I never looked that pasty. I needed some sun. I pinched my cheeks hard, trying to bring back some color and perhaps still trying to see if it was all a dream.

"Delores, come on down. Please. We don't have much time."

I couldn't put if off any longer. I emerged from the bathroom and took my trash bag of clothes back to the room. I threw it on the bed where I'd slept the night before. As swollen and raw as my eyes were, I knew there was no way to hide that I'd been crying. I stopped and stood in stillness for a few moments. I absorbed everything around me again, to convince myself I wasn't dreaming. My brain couldn't comprehend what was happening. I breathed in deeply. I had to face it. I twisted my hair into a big disheveled bun without even trying to comb it. Then, I slowly walked down the stairs. Everything in that house was too perfect. Who were these people? Who lives like this? I wondered.

I didn't know my way around the house, so I followed the smell of waffles and bacon. I came around the corner, and there was the blonde lady and two little kids maybe four or five years old. The perky lady's hair was pulled into a high pony tail with the help of a pink scrunchy. She was wearing a pink t-shirt, jean Capri overalls, and crispy white Keds. The kids looked almost identical to her, just smaller. Although a boy and a girl, they still might have been twins.

"Hi," the kids exclaimed in unison.

"Hi, back."

"I'm Jenny."

"I'm Josh."

"Welcome to our house. It's fun. You'll like it," Jenny said. Josh nodded enthusiastically in agreement.

The mom gestured for me to sit down and handed me a plate loaded up with eggs, waffles, and bacon. There was enough food on the plate for at least three people. I accepted the food and sat down. The lady then escorted the little kids out of the room.

"I need to be outside with them while they wait for their carpool. Be right back."

I sat alone at the large wood table. It had intricately carved legs and was surrounded by eight matching chairs. The weight of my isolation made me feel like I was drowning in that huge empty room. I tried to take a bite of bacon; admittedly it smelled really good. I felt the lump in my throat build again. Fighting back tears, I tried to swallow. I couldn't stop the tears from flowing. I wanted to throw my plate, but instead I sat there staring at the family photos that lined the walls around the table. The mom eventually came back and sat down next to me. She started to reach out to put a hand on my shoulder but stopped herself.

"It's going to be ok." She said in an almost whisper. I could tell she didn't believe it herself. She stood up and again quietly said, "Let's go talk with your caseworker. She can help you. You can leave your stuff here."

"Can I bring my backpack?" I asked.

"Of course."

I ran upstairs to grab it, I thought about bringing my bag too. I didn't want to lose anything else. Reluctantly I left it where it was. She stood outside the bedroom door waiting, hinting we were in a hurry. Then, in silence, we walked through a long hallway to a door that opened into the garage. The garage was bigger than most of the apartments I had lived in – cleaner too. Everything was perfectly organized. The shelves contained labeled bins and labeled peg boards lined the walls so even the hammer wouldn't get put away incorrectly. I could not have felt more out of place.

The perky lady unlocked the car door with her clicker, and we climbed in. She started the car by pushing a button. She didn't even have to put the key in it. Then she used another remote to open the garage door. The car was so quiet I couldn't tell if it was on. We pulled out into a subdivision with perfectly manicured lawns and flower beds. Then we made our way in silence across town. As we drove across the bridge to where the caseworker's office was, I saw the beautiful snowcapped mountain that my mom and I loved so much, peeking out from behind the clouds.

My mom and I always said that any day the mountain was out, was a good day. Today was not a good day. I wondered if my mom even knew what had happened.

15

# II

# A CASE NUMBER

WE SAT FOR about an hour and a half on uncomfortable metal chairs with faded primary blue upholstery on the seat and back. The silence between us was even more uncomfortable than the chairs. CPS confiscated my cell phone when they extracted me up from my friend's. I had no way to contact anyone and nothing to do while sitting and waiting. I felt trapped. I thumbed through some of the magazines that were arranged on the orange plastic table at the end of the rows of chairs. I wanted to look busy to keep people from trying to talk to me. My head was pounding – probably because of the harsh fluorescent lights and the lack of sleep and coffee. The severity of the light was made worse because it bounced off the white walls and white tiled floor. Both had black scuffs all over them; I wondered when the walls were painted last. These are the kinds of things that pop into your mind when you are sitting in a room like that for so long. Framed motivational posters lined the wall. An orange tabby kitten hanging from a branch "Hang in there" the poster summoned. Thanks for that. Everything is so much better now.

"Delores and Becky, your caseworker can see you now."

That's how I found out the perky lady's name. I really could not remember it, but I was too embarrassed to ask her. The door next to the receptionist opened, and a stereotypical social worker looking woman opened the door. She wore Dansko clogs, cream thick tights, a flowered skirt, cardigan sweater, and a scarf around her neck. She was perhaps in her late 20s or early 30s, had dark round glasses and her red hair was in a short pixie cut. She smiled a little too widely when she greeted us. She acted more like she was reuniting with an old friend than like she was just meeting a teen whose life she was about to destroy. She extended her hand and I politely shook it. It felt clammy and limp.

"Hi, my name's Sunny," she said. I thought, how perfect for the northwest. I guess her mom was feeling optimistic the day "Sunny" was born. Sunny's office was towards the end of the hall, most of the doors along the way were shut. I wondered who was inside each office. And how they were dealing with their own nightmares. As we walked, she and Becky chatted rapidly.

"How are the kids?" Sunny asked.

"They're great. They love their little school so much. They are both taking dance and music lessons too. How's your puppy? Have you been out hiking much?"

It seemed they knew each other well. Sunny unlocked the door to her office and we all squeezed in. Her office was decorated with pictures of her hiking with her puppy and friends, carefully placed between more motivational posters that look like they'd on the wall since at least the 1990s. She pointed at the chairs and said, "Please make yourselves comfortable."

I promised myself I would be strong and would not cry. Hoping that by that point all my tears had gone anyway.

Sunny asked me all the questions the other social worker asked the night before.

"Why were you missing so much school? Why were you staying in that apartment? Where's your mom?"

She kept asking about my mom and acted like she thought I was purposely lying about where she was. I told her all the places I thought she might be.

"She must be in one of the tent cities. You can probably find her there. Or sometimes she goes to the library downtown to use the computers – usually in the morning right when they open. She also uses the needle exchange, so maybe look for her when that's open?"

Didn't they realize I wanted to find her as much as they did? We generally didn't go more than a week or so without seeing each other. But I needed her right then. Next, the questions about my dad started.

"So, where's your dad? Does he know what's going on? Why doesn't he take care of you? When was the last time you saw him?"

"He's gone because of people like you," I screeched at Sunny. I couldn't hold back my anger.

She whispered to me to lower my voice and then she leaned back in her chair and took a deep breath.

"Help me understand what you mean by that, Delores."

"You really don't know? Don't you have some kind of database where you track everything about all of us?"

"Let me help you," she responded. Silence filled the room for what seemed like hours. "My dad was deported and has never been allowed to come back." I said finally, choking on the words.

"Ok, so staying with your dad isn't an option."

Wait, what? I remember being completely horrified. I told her my *papi* was deported and she just moved on to the next check box on her *pinche* form.

"Do you understand why foster care might be the best option to get the help you need?" Sunny asked.

"I'm fine. I can handle being on my own. If you want me to stop missing school, I can do that. No problem. I'll just go."

It was during that meeting that I pieced together that my school called CPS. I couldn't figure out which teacher or who in the school noticed I was gone. All my classes had so many kids; how did they even know I was missing? It just seemed pointless to go. I wasn't learning anything anyway. Guess that was a huge mistake. CPS probably never would have known I was on my own – if only I had gone to school.

"We've been trying to find your mom, but it's essential that you are in a safe, stable and nurturing environment," Sunny said.

"I swear, my mom never abused me. She loves me and is really nice to everyone. If you gave her a chance, even you'd love her. She is just having some troubles that she needs to work through."

"The school called not because of abuse but because they suspected neglect. Even though they didn't know you weren't living with your mom, they were concerned about you not going to school. They said when you did go you always wore the same thing and not the right kind of jacket," Sunny said.

"What does that even mean? Who pays attention to what I wear? And why does having a ton of clothes mean the person has better parents?"

"Do you think your mom can take care of you?" Sunny asked.

"Of course," then in a whisper, I admitted "but not right now. She is having troubles." I felt like I just ratted her out. But it was true she needed some help; it wasn't her fault. I love her so much. But I wanted her to get some help.

"Delores, are you listening to me?"

"Uh sorry no, what did you say?"

"Becky's house is only for when children first enter foster care. She isn't set up as a long-term home."

Then I was informed that the next steps in my "case" were to try to locate my mom and find me a "placement." I could stay with Becky for a few more days, but they needed to get me to a home prepared for teenagers. I also needed to get back to school. Sunny said she would "do her best" to keep me in the same school. She didn't bother to ask if that's what I wanted.

"Can I have my cell phone?"

"It's for the best that you don't have it right now. We need to keep you safe."

"But my mom will probably message me, and then I can tell her to call you. Please give me my phone. I know my friends are worried about me." I felt panicked.

"It's not your job to tell her to call us. We will continue trying to contact her." At that point, Sunny closed the file folder that contained all the information she was gathering about me signaling the meeting was over.

"We should hear something in a couple of days about where you will be transferred to. In the meantime, you should try to enjoy a nice long weekend," Sunny insisted.

19

# III

# THE SUBURBS

Becky and her children tried to act like my being in their house was normal, but I could tell they weren't quite sure what to say to me. Apparently, Becky's husband had some kind of tech job and traveled frequently. I never met him. We spent a lot of time shuttling the kids from one kind of lesson to another. Becky wasn't supposed to leave me alone, so I rode along wherever they went. The kids chattered amongst themselves, Becky listened to NPR, and I watched the rain roll down the windows. That was, when we were not in an area where I thought I might see my mom. Then, I scoured the streets hoping to spot her. Since it was the weekend, we hadn't heard anything back from the social worker. I didn't know if they found my mom – if I would get to be with her, and if not, where I would live next. Sometimes I was so pissed off. I wanted to lash out at Becky, but I could tell she was trying to make me feel better. I know none of it was her fault. But her perkiness was damn annoying.

One night on the way back to Becky's from her kids' lessons, she asked what we wanted for dinner. The kids scream in unison "PIZZA." Admittedly, pizza sounded good. I didn't feel hungry, but I realized I hadn't eaten much in about three days. Not that Becky didn't offer, I just couldn't get food past the lump in my throat. I hate to cry in front of people, so the best thing for me to do was to keep my mouth shut. Otherwise, the tears flowed.

"Can you order while I drive? Then we can pick it up on the way back to the house." Becky said as she handed me her cell phone.

"Sure. What do you guys want?"

"Pesto Primo and Brooklyn Bridge" the kids exclaimed, again speaking in unison. It was a little creepy. I guessed those were their favorites.

"I have no idea what those are. But, let's go with it."

"Yay"

I was really surprised when Becky ran in to get the pizza and left me in the car with her kids. I know "they" told her not to leave me alone and that I was a "runaway risk." I assume they thought that because I had been couch surfing and not living with my mom? For about a second, I considered taking off but since I don't know how to drive and didn't have any place to go – I stayed put.

The rain was coming down hard. Becky ran back to the car with the two huge pizza boxes. Even though she put them in the trunk, the smell filled the car. My stomach started growling immediately. The kids excitedly negotiated about what movie we should watch.

"Pizza night is the only night we are allowed to watch TV while eating," beamed Jenny.

"Every other night, we eat together as a family," Josh explained.

My family used to have pizza night too. It didn't happen often because mom usually worked evening shifts at the restaurant, but when she had off, we would order pizza and snuggle up on the sofa together. My *papi* loved watching kids movies because he said it helped him improve his English. I think it was just his excuse – because he didn't think tough guys should love kids movies as much as he did.

Back at Becky's house, she started the movie and the kids brought me a plate overflowing with pizza.

"We want to watch the movie with you. We picked *Coco* because we want to learn about México," Jenny exclaimed.

"Ok, sounds like a plan. I haven't seen it either."

Apparently, Becky told them my dad is Mexican. Honestly, I kind of enjoyed being around the kids. They were cute and it was nice to hear their frequent laughter. I settled into the ginormous white sofa, with built-in recliners and cup holders in front of the massive flat screen TV. Becky ate one piece of pizza and then went to the adjoining room and sat at her computer during the rest of the movie.

After the movie, the kids started asking tons of questions about México. Most of them I couldn't answer. I had barely been out of Seattle, let alone to México.

Then the line of questioning got more personal, "Your mom's white, like us, right? Is that why your skin isn't as dark as some of the people in the movie? How much Spanish do you talk? Where's your dad? Does your grandma look like Mama Coco?"

"Ok, that's probably enough questions for tonight," Becky said. "It's time for bed." I saw that as my opportunity to hide in the bedroom.

"I'm tired too," I announced.

I was relieved that the questioning had ended. I know they were just curious, and I really liked them...but it was still a little overwhelming.

Early the next morning, I woke up to the sound of several adult voices and sobbing. I wanted to know what was going on, but also kind of didn't. Even after the other adults left and I could only hear Becky and the kids, I stayed in bed for as long as I could. Finally, I needed to pee, so I ran to the bathroom. As I looked in the mirror, I gave myself a pep talk. I splashed water on my face to try to take away the tiredness and the dark circles rimming my green eyes. You can do this, I told myself as wove my hair into two thick braids. I pulled on the hoodie. Go see what's happening. You have to be brave. You have to take care of yourself. Big Breath. Ok, here I go.

I slowly walked to the kitchen. As I came around the corner, I saw a teen girl – who looked a little older than me – sitting at the table. She was wearing a purple hoodie and it was pulled tightly around her head. She looked up when she heard me enter and muttered, "Hey." Her eyes were all puffy.

"Hey, back," I said trying to force a smile. She looked so sad, I immediately wanted to help and comfort her.

Becky was busily cooking pancakes. She turned around and told me, "Janae will also be staying with us for a few days."

"Cool," I responded.

What an odd response. But what else could I have said? I assumed that Janae's life was currently as fucked up as mine. We sat together in silence. I ate my pancakes and bacon, remembering how I could barely get food past the lump in my throat just a few days ago. Occasionally, Janae and my eyes met. I could sense that she was having a similar experience to my first day. I wanted to tell her it gets better, but I wasn't sure if that was true.

"If you want to talk, I'll listen," I offered.

Janae nodded. Her beautiful obsidian eyes filled with tears. I handed her a napkin from the table. She took it and buried her face. I reached out and touched her shoulder. She leaned into me and sobbed. Becky remained silent and busied herself with cooking and cleaning.

"Hey, can we go listen to some music?" I asked Becky.

"Sure for a few minutes, while I get the kids ready. Then we need to go run some errands. You'll have to come with, since I can't leave you at the house alone."

I honestly think I would have gone crazy during my time at Becky's house if it wasn't for her adorable little kids. They were goofy, welcoming, and unguarded. I guess they were used to having teens come through their house. So, it was their "normal." They talked non-stop while we ran around town, which meant Janae and I were off the hook. At the end of the day, Janae and I were finally alone to talk about how we ended up at Becky's.

"They made me leave my last foster home because my foster mom had a baby and decided she couldn't foster anymore," Janae shared.

"That's awful. I'm so sorry."

"Yeah, well you know what they say – finding homes for teenagers is almost impossible."

"Yup, I've definitely heard that at least a hundred times already."

"My caseworker says she has been trying to find a new placement for a while, but no one will take me because of my age. Once the baby came, they picked

23

me up and brought me here. I didn't even get to see the baby before they moved me. My last house wasn't the best place in the world and I'd much rather be with my mom, but I was so relieved to be out of those damn group homes. It was better for sure. I'd been with Lilian, my foster mom, for almost two years. I guess I thought they'd keep me until I graduated at the end of this year. I even offered to help with the baby. But apparently, Lilian's boyfriend wanted it to be just their family. So here I am."

# IV

# CRAVING FREEDOM

ON WEDNESDAY, SUNNY called to tell me they found my mom.

"We confirmed that your mom is homeless and still using heroin. Under those circumstances we aren't allowed to release you to her care."

In that moment, I hated my mom for putting me in such a horrible situation. I hated being in foster care more. Even though I was pissed off at my mom, I wanted to be with her. I didn't understand why she didn't just get her shit together. I mean, I know getting off junk is super hard – but she is a strong woman. She wasn't always like that! I knew she could get better. I was totally fucked.

After giving me the heart wrenching news that I would not be going back with my mom, Sunny told me she found a group home that would take me.

"I will pick you up from Becky's after school tomorrow to take you to your new placement. Please be ready at 4:30." She was cold and robotic as she dictated what would happen in my life.

"Ok," I replied reluctantly.

I was terrified. The only thing I knew about the new "placement" was that it was a group home for teen girls and that I was expected to go back to my old school. The same school that turned me in to CPS. What could possibly go wrong? That night Becky ordered pizza and her kids tried to cheer me up. Both of them drew pictures of me in México as parting gifts. They said they tried hard to make it look like the movie *Coco*. I wondered if I would ever see the kids or Janae again. Janae was super quiet the whole night, she hadn't heard anything about where she would be going next.

She told me earlier that she wanted to graduate from her current school, since she was close to being done. Janae was getting taxi vouchers because her school was across town from Becky's. However, once she got a permanent placement, she might have to transfer.

"The thought of changing schools again is too much," Janae mumbled.

"I'm so sorry, I really hope things work out and you can graduate with your friends. Don't give up. Keep telling the social worker what you want."

My heart ached. When everyone was getting ready for bed Becky asked to talk to me for a minute privately. We walked down to the kitchen and she offered me a cup of sleepy time tea.

"You can do this," she said. "I know it's really hard. I can also tell by the way you interact with the kids and try to help Janae that you have a kind heart. You're smart too. You can make choices about what happens next. You can choose to make your life better or worse."

"Ok," is all I could think to say in response.

"I have a little something for you," and with that she pulled out a pink and black checkered duffle bag that was large enough for all my stuff.

"Thank you so much. That's really thoughtful. I'm going to go pack."

I wondered if she had a supply of duffle bags for these moments. How many kids came to her house with their stuff in trash bags? I didn't ask because I was a little afraid that if I knew how many kids were in my shoes, I would have felt even worse. Janae was sleeping (or pretending she was) by the time I got to the bedroom. As quietly as possible, I stuffed everything into my new duffle bag. Then I climbed into bed. I don't know if I actually slept.

The next morning everyone in the house acted like things were normal, until it was time for Janae to leave for school. We hugged each other so tightly I am surprised one of us didn't end up with a broken rib. We didn't know if we'd see each other again or where we'd end up. We had only known each other for a few days but they were some of the most intense days in our young lives. The taxi honked and we forced ourselves apart.

"Be ok," Janae implored.

"You too," I replied as I wiped a stray tear. I never saw her again. She would be just one of the many people that came rushing into and out of my life over the next few years.

During the next several of months, I ran away from every group home they put me in. Group homes are the worst. After being caught for about the third or fourth time, I ended up in a group home that was more like a prison than a home. They checked my shoes every time I walked in the door – suspecting that I had drugs on me. They gave me random pee tests because I was known for smoking a bunch of weed. And I had to hide my cigarettes in my bra! I felt like a criminal. They even locked the cupboards so we couldn't get to the food. I absolutely hated it there. I never had so many restrictions in my whole life. They dictated everything – what time we woke up, ate, watched TV, did homework, and showered. Everything. They also didn't trust us. We weren't allowed to do our own laundry, cook, or go to the store. Everything worked on a point system. Once I got enough points, I could earn a bus pass, and would be allowed to go to school by myself. The house mom or one of the workers drove me to school and picked me up. I felt like I was suffocating.

After what seemed like forever, they finally let me have my phone but only for an hour a day, AND I had to be in the common room when I had it. Most of the time when my mom got to the library or borrowed a phone to try to message me, I didn't have my phone and couldn't chat with her. They also made me give them my passwords; they said it was for my "protection." I worried that one of my friends would message something that would get me in even more trouble. I had absolutely no privacy. The lack of privacy was worse than when I was couch surfing.

The caseworker, the lawyer, the house mom, and the school said they were just trying to help me, but I felt like I'd been criminalized. Rather than being treated like a kid who needed a circle of support, I was treated like a felon. What was I doing that was so awful? What justified them treating me that way? Yeah, I skipped school, and I smoked a little mota, but it helped me feel better. Sometimes I got so sad or anxious – smoking a little weed made it more manageable.

I hated sharing a room with three other girls. We had eight girls total in that house. There were two bunk beds in each room and a long closet where everyone had to store their clothes. We also had a plastic bin for our personal items, which didn't exactly keep our things safe from being stolen by the other inmates (or "residents" as the staff called us). Most of the girls fought with each other constantly, and someone was stealing clothes and makeup. It was crazy there – I walked into the room on one night and my roommates were screaming at each.

"You're such a bitch, give it back." Tina, a muscular short girl with bright blue hair, screamed.

"Make me." Julia demanded while holding a sweater over her head. Julia must have been at least 6 feet tall. The next day when I got home, they were giggling and sitting on the same bed like they were best friends. That was typical of the chaos in the house. There was constant drama. It made everything more stressful and terrible.

Most of the girls had been there for a while. They formed packs. The Spanish speaking girls hung together, as did the white girls. The one Black girl didn't say much. I can only imagine how alienated she felt. People generally pass me off as white (until I get some sun on my skin). I didn't let on that I spoke Spanish, I just observed and tried to keep off everyone's radar. I figured the less the others noticed me, the better. I was so tired. I knew I had to figure out how to get out and stay out of there.

I had so many caseworkers since Sunny, I can't remember all of their names. I kept asking the caseworkers if I could move someplace else.

"You know you are considered a high risk of running, so no foster home will accept you. You made those decisions and now you have to live with the consequences. You also have to fully commit to not smoking marijuana. Until then we cannot place you in a normal foster home," the young fresh social worker replied. She then reminded me for at least the millionth time that teens are hard to place.

"I guess I am stuck," I sighed. At that moment, I decided to do everything they told me to for a while so I could get enough points to have some freedom.

All of us, in the group home, were in high school. Most of us were behind in our credits for graduation, so tutors came to work with us after school. Luckily, school was generally easy for me, so I earned a couple credits pretty fast. I didn't care about school, but doing good kept them off my back a little. I was frustrated because they didn't seem to have any idea about which classes I actually needed to graduate. They changed my schedule three times since they put me in the new school. Part of the problem is that there were too many kids at the school, so the classes I needed were already full and they needed to put me somewhere. They also wouldn't believe me when I told them what I already knew.

We had a team meeting with the foster mom from the group home, the school counselor, the assistant principle and myself to try to fix my schedule. The meeting went something like this.

"I already know algebra," I insisted.

"Your grades say otherwise, the records from your last school say you earned a D," the bushy eyebrowed and badly dressed school counselor said.

"That's because I didn't do the homework, because I already knew how to do it. Look at my tests – they were all A's."

"We have to go on what the grade's say, and the grade says you haven't mastered algebra," the assistant principal said. He insisted we all call him, "Mr. Williams." He had a comb-over and still wore a suit and tie to work. Who even does that anymore? He seemed ancient and didn't even try to understand where I was coming from.

"That is the stupidest thing I ever heard," I blurted out.

"Don't be so snarky. If you know algebra so well, the class should be very easy," Mr. Williams replied.

"Sure, it will be easy, but isn't that a total waste of my time?" I asked trying to remain calm. Apparently, whether or not things made sense wasn't his concern. It took less than five minutes to understand that he already didn't like me for whatever reason he cooked up.

For the next few weeks, I forced myself to jump through all their hoops. I did all my homework, passed all my tests, got up on time, and even stopped sneaking *mota*. I passed the random drug tests – twice. The house mom praised me and told my social worker that I was finally settling in. Were they really that dumb? Did they think that all the sudden I resolved myself to life in a group home and thought it was awesome? I cannot believe that behind the smile they didn't realize how deeply miserable I was. I guess it doesn't matter what they thought was happening – because it worked. I got my bus pass and permission to go to school by myself. For a couple of days, I packed a few extra clothes in my backpack before heading to school. I was afraid they might notice if I stuffed it with everything I would need all at one time. I even managed to smuggle out the duffle bag that Becky gave me. I didn't have a plan for which day I would flee. I just knew I would not stay at that place. I waited it out and when the time was right, I made my move.

The school loved to have assemblies to "build school spirit." Everyone hated them. You could tell the nerdy kids and the principal planned them because they were so out of touch with the rest of our lives. Cheesy doesn't begin to describe them. Proof that I am not the only one that hated them came when the fire alarm went off about ten minutes into the principal's pep-talk. Perfect chaos ensued since all the practice alarms happened when students were in home-room, not at an assembly. This was my chance. I filed out of the gym with every-one else. The crowded hallways offered the cover I needed to get to my locker and grab my stuff, which was already in the duffle bag. I am pretty short so it was easy to hide in the crowd. Even with the large duffle bag, I went unnoticed.

By the time I got out of the building, students packed the sidewalk. I slipped into the crowd gathered in front of the bus stop. Just then a bus pulled up; I jumped on without even looking at which direction it was headed. It didn't matter. All that mattered was that I was free again.

# V

# ON THE STREETS

MY HEART WAS beating frantically. I could hear it in my ears. I felt like I was going to pass out. It would take at least three hours before I was reported missing to my social worker. I had no idea what I was going to do next. I needed a place to stay where they couldn't find me. And I needed to get my hands on a cell phone. I also had no money. I could do without food for a couple of days, but the phone I needed. I needed to find my mom asap.

I knew I couldn't go back to the friend's house I was staying at when they took me before. I wasn't sure who would be willing to help me hide or who thought I was safer in foster care and would turn me in. It was winter and too cold to sleep on the street. I knew lots of people were doing it. I didn't want to, though. I didn't pay attention to where the bus was taking me. I completely spaced out until I realized we were almost to the airport. I pulled the cord for the next stop. Then, I walked until I found a place to cross over to the other side of the highway. I needed to head back north into the city to find some help.

I remembered one of my mom's old friends telling me that if I ever needed anything I could count on her. We hadn't seen her in a couple of years, but I figured she still lived in the same spot. She always seemed so stable. She and my mom were really close – before everything went wrong. I think Tina loves her but couldn't handle seeing my mom destroy her life. I assumed she had no idea I was in foster care. She wouldn't know to turn me in. Good plan, I thought. I headed for her house. It took three buses and almost four hours to get to her neighborhood.

I didn't remember the exact address but knew I was close. I walked up and down the streets looking for clues that I had found the right house. I spotted a huge Douglas fir with a fountain underneath. Next to the fountain was a knee-high Quan Yin statue, lightly covered in moss. It made the stone statue more beautiful and assured me that I had found Tina's house. I remembered the time that my mom, Tina, and I had gone to the art museum. Tina told me about Quan Yin, as we walked by statues and paintings of her. Quan Yin is the goddess of compassion. Tina loves her. I could smell garlic and rice cooking.

I walked up the stone pathway to the humble salmon colored bungalow with the covered porch. I lightly knocked on the door and then gathered the courage to knock harder.

"Just a sec," A women's voice responded. A moment later, Tina opened the door and looked at me quizzically, with a mixture of surprise and uncertainty.

"It's me, Didi."

Tina gasped and pulled me into a massive bear hug. Next came a string of questions. "How are you? Where is your mom? How have you been? When did you get so tall? Are you hungry? Oh my god, why are we standing in the rain? Come in."

Over the next couple of hours, I filled Tina in about what had happened to mom and me. I left out the part about me being taken into foster care. Tina is one of those people that follows the rules, and I know she would feel like she had to turn me in. If she didn't know, then she would not have that decision to make.

"Can I stay with you for a couple of days? Just until I can find my mom." I finally got up the courage to ask.

"Of course. I told you when you were little that you could always count on me. You can stay in the guest room. Let me just get my stuff off the bed. I just got back from a trip and threw everything in there. Why don't you grab some stir-fry from the stove? I always make too much anyway."

"Thank you, Tina. I missed you. It's so good to see you."

Tina hugged me again and kissed me on both cheeks. She is one of those people that you can't help to love hugging even if you don't normally like it. She hugs with all of her heart. After dinner, we chatted a bit more and then she said she was tired from her trip and needed to get some sleep. She had to get up at 6:00 am for work.

The next day, I woke up at about noon. I couldn't believe I slept for 13 hours straight. I went out to the kitchen and found a note from Tina.

"Hey love, I didn't want to wake you. I should be home from work by about 6:30. Make yourself at home. Here's a key for you, please lock up if you go anywhere. XOXOXOXO"

I burst into tears when I read the word home. I missed having a home so *pinche* much. Freedom and a home. Shouldn't everyone have this?

I took a deep breath to hold back the panic. I looked around and like most Northwesterners Tina had at least three different ways to make coffee. I decided on the French press. I would need to be fully caffeinated to face the day. While the coffee was steeping, I jumped in the shower. It felt so strange to be alone in a house with no one looking over me. It was almost too quiet. After the shower, I turned on the radio. It was set to NPR. Does everyone in this town listen to NPR? I sat on Tina's big comfy round brown velvet chair and drank my coffee. I watched the rain roll slowly down the window pane. It seemed like forever ago since I had the luxury of slowly sipping coffee, listening to music, and watching the rain. My thoughts were interrupted when a huge black and white fluffy cat jumped into my lap. The moment was perfect. I wished it could last forever and that it could be my normal.

I spent way more time petting that gorgeous cat than I should have, but I couldn't find the energy to go look for my mom that day. After I finished my coffee, I took a nap instead. I jumped up when I heard the front door open. How could I have slept so long? I was embarrassed when Tina asked me what I did during the day.

"Honey, we all get tired. Sometimes we need to rest." She gave me a giant hug and then she said, "I brought Thai food for dinner. Is vegetarian, ok?'

No wonder my mom liked her so much when I was little. Tina was just about one of the nicest people I have ever met. I wonder why she wasn't married and if she had a boyfriend. It seemed kind of rude to ask though, so I didn't. She seemed to like her life just as it was. I wondered if I would ever have that. Would it be possible for me to be content and happy in my lifetime? I wished that for my mom as well.

# VI

# SEARCHING

I SPENT ANOTHER couple of nights at Tina's, but then she started asking a lot of questions. "Let's come up with a plan to find your mom. What will you and your mom do for housing? Aren't you going to get into trouble for missing so much school?"

It was awesome being with her, but I knew I had to go. At some point she would realize that I belonged to the state and she would make that dreaded call. I left her a note.

"Thank you for everything. Don't worry. Love, Didi"

I planned to find my mom, and when we were back on our feet, I would let Tina know. It seems kind of mean now – I know she worried, but none of our mess was her problem. I had to figure it out on my own.

For lack of a better option, I took the bus down to a street by the university that everyone in town just calls "the Ave." A lot of street kids hang out there. I knew some of them from other times I ran away. I saw an old friend, Mike, sitting under the awning trying to stay out of the rain. Mike was much taller than me and had black hair that defied gravity and stuck straight up. He was wearing old brown lace up boots, a pink T-shirt, and an army jacket that was too big for him. He was with a few other teens and they were all panhandling. They looked a little rough with their wild DIY haircuts and dirty clothes, but I figured it was better to be with a group on the streets than to be alone. I walked over and plopped myself down next to Mike.

"Hey, what's up? Where you been?" he asked.

"Things have been shitty," I responded.

"Wanna feel better?" he asked, as he pulled out a small glass one-hitter and handed it to me.

It was the first time in weeks I smoked *mota*. Although it didn't make my problems go away, it helped make things feel not so overwhelming. The weed wasn't nearly as comforting as coffee in Tina's huge round chair, with that purring fluffy cat on my lap. As we sat on the sidewalk and smoked, the dampness and cold felt daunting. I had no idea when I would sleep inside again. The longer we sat the more kids joined us. Some of them had tents down by the freeway; they told me they didn't like the tent cities and felt safer in spots where only teens hung out. Mike was crashing at his girlfriend's aunt's house, but a couple other kids invited me to stay with them.

"We don't have much room in our tent, but you can crash with us until you find your mom," Joe said. He was a lanky kid with drab long blonde hair who always had a skateboard in his hand or nearby.

"Yeah, totally, we have been out here for almost a year. It's good to hook up with people that know how to survive. There are a lot of cool people on the streets but some rotten ones too. You gotta be smart," Elisa added. She and Joe were first loves, and had been together for a few years by then. Elisa usually wore her ginger hair in two braids, topped with one of those multicolored long knit elf-style hats. She played with the pink puff on the end while she talked.

Joe and Elisa looked tired and in need of showers, but overall, pretty ok. I didn't have another option and figured being in a tent with them would at least be warm.

"Ok, cool. Thanks. I should be able to find my mom tomorrow and then this will all be over."

Several of the other kids, who I met on the streets, were runaways from foster care too. Most of their parents were addicted to something or in jail. Except for the gay kids. Several of them were on the streets because their parents told them to "stop being gay, or leave." That just blew my mind. I'll never understand how a parent can throw their kid out. I think I felt the worst for them. For the rest of us, shit happened – life didn't go as planned. We need to figure out how to move on and deal with it the best we can. But for some of the gay kids, their parents had nice houses, steady jobs, and everything. They could have given their kids the world, but chose not to. It is really fucked up and tragic.

For the next few days, I rode the busses from one tent city to another. Sometimes Joe or Elisa would come with me to keep me company and to help me stay brave while talking to strung out people and the gatekeepers. They were intimidating at times, but I understand why people were nervous about outsiders. Our city is dripping with money but turned its back on the working and middle class, the poor, and the sick. Everyone acts like the homeless people are the problem, instead of acknowledging the real problems – no affordable housing, not being able to get mental health care, and overflowing substance abuse treatment centers. While I was staying at Tina's, I read in the local paper that to afford a two-bedroom apartment the average person must work 93 hours a week or over 2 full time jobs at minimum wage.

Is it really a mystery how mom and I ended up couch surfing? She worked her ass off until her back was so jacked she couldn't work anymore. She often worked double shifts at the restaurant and would come home and pass out, wake up in the morning and race off for another early morning shift. She tried so hard to take care of me by herself after they deported my *papi*. I know many of the people in the tent cities have similar stories.

It was depressing and sometimes terrifying going into the tent cities looking for my mom. It was also heartbreaking. After a few days of searching, I found out where my mom was staying. The gatekeeper was a grey-haired man wearing an old ball cap that said "Proud Veteran." He had a huge scar on his face and walked with a limp.

"I'm looking for my mom. Her name is Courtney. She's little taller than me and has straight long blonde hair."

"You, Didi? She talks about you a lot. She should be around after 7 or so. Come back then," he said.

"Yeah, I'm Didi. Please tell her I am coming. I'll be back tonight. Thank you, thank you."

"Sure thing, kid."

I didn't even want to think about what she was doing during the day. It only takes one bad hit, and you're dead. The conversations Elisa, Joe and I had about heroin flooded my brain.

"A lot of people OD'd in the last couple of weeks. Fentanyl is hitting our streets hard. The junkies know the risks but when they are sick, they just want to get better. They take chances – sometimes they die." Elisa's words from a few nights before haunted me.

"Activists are trying to get safe injection sites here, but of course, people are trying to keep them from happening. They think the sites will bring more drugs into town. Stupidity. This town already has tons of drugs. The safe injection sites might keep needles from being all over the damn streets. They would save lives for sure."

Joe ranted some version of this frequently. He had lost three friends and his uncle to heroin in the last couple of years. He always told the kids on the streets to stay away from it. "Weed only" was his motto. He didn't even drink alcohol. "It's poison," he said.

I knew everyone looked down at my mom, as if they were better than her. It pissed me off more than it embarrassed me, because they were so smug. They don't realize that if one too many horrible things happened to them – their life could go this way too. None of us are immune to tragedy.

# VII

# FINDING MOM

I T TOOK A lot of convincing to get Mike to come with me to meet up with my mom. He tries to act tough, but the truth is a lot of the street kids are kind of afraid of the street adults. Going to a place that is mostly adults is something they often avoid. He also didn't have any money for the bus, but I told him I'd talk the driver into letting him ride for free. Luckily, my bus pass from the last group home was still working. I guess they can't deactivate it?

When we boarded the bus, I swiped my card. Then I smiled widely and begged the driver not to charge Mike.

"Please, please, please, let my friend come with me. He doesn't have any money but I am afraid to go downtown by myself at night. Just this once, please!" There was a long line forming behind us and the bus was standing room only.

"Get in," the driver said. "I suspect you won't take no without out a fight, and I need to keep on schedule. But you need to pay me next time you get on my bus. Got me."

"*Claro y muchas gracias*," I replied.

"*De nada*," he replied – finally smiling.

I suspected he was Latino. I thought a little Spanish might help the situation. Of course, we all knew that Mike wouldn't have money next time either.

We squeezed our way into the middle of the bus and stood sandwiched between all the students and tech-bros heading towards the gentrified sections of downtown. They were likely going out for an overpriced meal or some lame sportsball event. They avoided eye contact with us and pulled themselves in tight to avoid touching our dirty clothes and unbathed bodies.

"Let's get off here and walk the rest of the way. I'm sick of being on this damn bus," Mike said.

"Gotcha. It smells like tech-money in here. It's scary," I replied.

The mist provided comfort as we walked towards the water and the tent city. I felt nauseous, I wasn't sure if it was from hunger or worry. I didn't know what condition my mom would be in or if she'd even be there yet. As we approached the entrance an extremely tall longshoreman looking man stopped us. He had a huge beard, broad shoulders and wore a yellow rain jacket and a black beanie.

"Hi, I'm Courtney's daughter, Didi. The old guy that was here earlier told me to come back and find her tonight."

"Wait here. And don't go past this point. I'll see if I can find her."

About fifteen minutes later my mom appeared. She had dark circles under her eyes and was really thin. She looked exhausted but relatively ok. I tried to play it cool, but as soon as she hugged me the tears began. I cried so hard my body shook.

"It'll be ok; it'll be ok," she kept repeating.

"How's it going to be ok?" I shrieked.

"I don't know." At that point, she cried and her voice lowered to a whisper.

Mike stepped away then so my mom and I could talk. The mist turned into a downpour.

"Can you walk with me a little, mom? I want to talk where no one is listening."

We walked holding hands for a couple of blocks, making no attempt to stay dry or to talk. The pain in our hearts was palpable. After a couple blocks, we ducked under the awning of a closed business.

"Please get help. Please. For me," I pleaded.

"I tried but the waiting lists are so long. And without insurance, it's impossible to get anyone to even talk to me. That's the first thing they ask. When I tell them I don't have insurance, they just say, 'Sorry, wish there was something we can do.' The social worker told me I have to do a million things before we can be together again. She said I need stable housing, and to successfully complete treatment, and to start counseling. I'm not even sure why I have to do that AND go to treatment. They are kind of the same thing, or so I thought. I feel so fucking hopeless. I don't even know where to start. I feel like they don't want me to get you back. I don't know how I can do this with no money."

The only jobs she ever had was in food service, but with her back injury she cannot carry trays anymore. Her bartending license was expired, and she couldn't afford to renew it. The social worker also said she didn't think bartending would be an "appropriate" job for someone who has "addiction issues."

"Have you asked the social worker for help?"

"Of course, but I feel like they are setting me up to fail. No one wants to help me do the things they are asking me to do. I told them I want treatment. They have this attitude that if I am going to be able to be a 'good mom' I have to do this on my own."

"*¡Chingá!* What are we going to do?"

"Honey, no one wants to be a junkie. Please, please, forgive me. I'm trying so damn hard. I just need a little help."

As she said these words, she rocked back and forth shuffling her feet and scratched at her arms. She looked at the ground instead of into my eyes. She always looked intensely in my eyes when talking to me...before life got out of control. She looked unequivocally defeated.

"Why don't you just quit?" I begged.

Even though I knew she would if she could. I also knew the pain in her back was brutal and that she gets really sick if she doesn't shoot up for a while. Then she is so out of it she can't even try to look for a job or meet with the social worker or anything. Knowing all this didn't make my frustration and fear any less.

"What about me? What am I supposed to do?"

"I think you should go back to the group home. At least there you'll be safe." She said, still not able to look at me.

"Mom, look at me. Do you really want me to be there instead of with you?"

"Being on the street is the worst place for you. Go to school, make something of yourself. You're so smart and can do anything you want." She finally looked into my eyes.

She sounded angry but her eyes filled with tears. I almost felt like my mom was saying good-bye. I was crushed. She used to be such a fighter. She was creative and hilarious, and no matter how hard things got she found a way. All that seemed to be gone from her now, she was just a shell of her former self. Even her stunning good looks were gone. She used to be the woman that would stop men (and some women) in their tracks. Now her hair and eyes were lifeless. She was wearing a thick black hoodie; I knew it hid the track marks and abscesses. Sometimes I hated her for letting smack consume her. Then, I felt sorry for her. I believed she wanted to get better, that she wanted her life back. I also believed that no one was actually trying to help her.

As I went from one tent city to another looking for her, I understood even more that those with power and money had turned their backs on everyone else. In a city that is near the top of the list for having the most billionaires, over 11,000 people are homeless. Heroin was all over our city, again. My mom and I were not alone in our struggles, but that didn't make them any *pinche* easier. Or less real.

I really didn't know what to say. It seemed like we were out of options.

"I promise to keep meeting with the social worker and trying to get a job. I know some people who got on methadone. I might be able to get on that."

We hugged each other tightly and cried. I saw Mike waiting down the street and motioned to him that it was ok to come back.

"I'll keep keep trying," she said as he approached.

We slowly walked back to her temporary home in the tent city. The sounds of the cars on the overpass, the sirens, and the horns mixed with the chatter in my head. There were no right words though, so we walked in silence. The strong smell of fish, fried food, and urine permeated the air, as it did most days in this part of town. The downpour hadn't washed the stench of the city away. The rain slowed as we arrived at the camp.

"You guys can stay here for the night, if you want?"

"No offense, but we'd rather be with other kids. Any chance you have money so Mike can get on the bus?"

"Yeah, I got some today." She reached in her pocket and gave us 5 bucks. I didn't ask where it came from.

"I love you, Didi. Please take care of yourself."

"I love you too, mom. And you take care of yourself. I worry about you out here. Seriously."

We hugged for what felt like a very long time and Mike finally put his hand on my shoulder and nodded his head towards the bus stop. Mom and I reluctantly released from our embrace. I turned and walked away. I couldn't bear to look back. My tears fell. I tried to fool myself that they would be hidden by the mist. Mike gave me an almost grandmotherly kiss on the top of my head and grabbed my hand. He had never showed any kind of affection. Guess he knew I needed it. I was exhausted and numb.

# VIII

# DREAMS

THE DAYS WENT by sluggishly when I lived on the streets. The sun didn't come up until almost eight and went down by a little after four. That gave me an excuse to tuck myself into a sleeping bag for much of the day. We also spent many hours begging on the Ave. Between all of us, we managed to get enough money for one pay as you go cell phone – mine had been turned off by then. We took turns checking our messages on that phone – trying to stay connected to anyone we could think of. It felt like if I didn't have a phone, I'd be forgotten. My mom sent me short messages a few times a week. At least now no one else had my password.

"The social worker asked if we've been seeing each other. I said no, of course. Be safe. I love you – Mom."

"Please go back to the group home. You will be safer there. I'm worried about you. I want to see you. Are you ok? Keep me posted. I love you – Mom"

"I'd rather be on the streets than feel like a prisoner," I responded. I knew I couldn't live like that forever though. I had to figure out something.

Some nights in the tent, we allowed ourselves to dream about the lives we wished we could live. It's hard to dream when you're trying so hard to survive.

"I want to go to México and be with my *papi*," I told Elisa and Joe.

"When I was little, my *papi* talked a lot about us all going to live in his *pueblo*. He wanted a *ranchito* with *burros*, horses, and chickens. *Papi* said our house would be bright orange and have a view of the mountains and a rooftop *mirador*, where we could sit and watch the sunset over the lake. I want to know mi *familia* – my *abuelos*, *tíos*, *tías*, and *primos*. I met one *tío*, that means uncle. You know that, right? Anyway, he came through Seattle after working in Alaska. He wanted to come back the next year too, but wasn't able to get across the border. My *papi* tried to come back a couple of times too, but didn't make it. Crossing the border has gotten too *pinche* dangerous for him to try again. My mom said she begged him not to cross, because she was afraid he would be killed. That's when he finally gave up."

"That's so fucked up," Joe said. "I wish we could all live anywhere we wanted."

"Borders are stupid," Elisa added.

I thought about my *papi* all the time. My aunt set up Facebook for him and he messaged me sometimes. Not too often though, he said he didn't like to spend time looking at that phone. He preferred to look at the mountains and the sky.

"*Mija, te extraño a ti y a tu mamá.* I hope you can both move to México and be with me. Tell your mom, I still love her." His last message said.

He always wrote in Spanglish. He knew I wanted to practice Spanish but he also wanted to practice English. He said he never got to use it anymore.

It was so sad. My *papi* remembered my mom the way she was. I didn't have the heart to tell him what happened to her. He told me she didn't respond to his messages any more. I told him she didn't like the phone either.

Most of the kids I was hanging with on the street hadn't ever left Seattle. They were fascinated when I told them about my dream to move to México. I shared stories with them that my *papi* shared with me. For a few moments, we got to be excited and had hope. One night while sitting on the hill staring down at I-5 we all talked about what we thought we would be when we grew up. All the usual answers – nurse, veterinarian, game developer, football player. Mike surprised us all when he said, as a child he wanted to be an astrophysicist.

My mom's words haunted the conversation, "no one wants to be a junkie." My mom wanted to be a lawyer. She struggled in school though, and her parents and teachers told her she wasn't meant for college. Unfortunately, she believed them and she never even applied.

The dreary days passed slowly. Each day basically the same. We tried to earn money, get food, and stay warm. Some days people were exceptionally kind to us and would buy us food or hot coffee. Other days, people were complete assholes. Sometimes people would yell at us when we asked them for money. I even had a frat boy spit on me. Sitting on the street, I watched wealth whiz past us. The amount of money people spend on cars and clothes boggles my mind. Mostly, you could tell that the people who walked by us thought they were immune to our situation. They believed it could never happen to them and that this was somehow our fault. I hated people who looked down at us. But even though they saw us as less than them, I never let myself believe that was true. I was determined to find a way out of the misery.

# IX

# JOY RIDE

OUR USUAL CREW was sitting on the sidewalk in front of a headshop on the Ave, once again trying to collect enough money to pay for our phone so we didn't lose our number. I whipped my head around because I thought I saw Mike drive past us.

"Whoa, is that Mike?" I gasped.

"Shit, I think so," Elisa responded.

"Where the hell did he get a van?" Joe asked.

Mike pulled into the 3-minute loading zone in front of the UW bookstore. He jumped out of a tri-tone brown vintage toaster-shaped van and yelled at us.

"Hey, you guys. Jump in. Let's go for a cruise."

We grabbed our backpacks and blankets from the sidewalk and ran to the van. As we climbed in, we bombarded him with questions. All of us talking at the same time. "Where'd you get this?" "Did you steal it?" "Seriously, dude, what's up?"

"My uncle told me I could have it if I could get it running again. He thought it might help me get a job, and at the very least, I'd always have a place to sleep. It has been sitting behind his barn up north for years."

"Dude, what year is it? It's so badass."

"It's a 1973 – Volkswagen, of course. It was pretty easy to figure out how to get it going again. My uncle John's wife hated this thing and has been trying to get him to get rid of it since they got married. She said it is dangerous, not environmentally friendly, and smells like hippies and dogs."

We all started cracking up. Some of it was valid. The crumbling upholstery smelled mostly of mold, but you could also faintly smell incense and weed. But we weren't judging – it had wheels and could easily sleep a few people. I immediately started thinking about what it would be like to sleep in it instead of in the tent with Joe and Elisa.

"Where should we go?" Mike said joyously.

"Let's go to México!" I responded.

"That might be a little far; I just got it running today. Let's see how it holds up on the way to Everett."

"¡Órale!"

"Can we go to the beach instead? Maybe just up to Edmonds?" Joe chimed in; the rest of us filled the van with cheers,

"Yep, it should make it there. My uncle also bought me a full tank of gas as my 'reward' for getting her going."

"¡Vámonos!," I yelled.

"Check it out it has an 8-track player! Does that even work?" Joe shrieked.

"Yeah, totally. My uncle gave me some of his old 8-tracks; they're in the bag behind your seat." Joe reached behind his seat and grabbed a red cloth bag filled with old 8-tracks.

"Ok, we have The Wall, Alice Cooper, and Kiss?"

"Fuck yeah! The Wall. Crank it"

The speakers rattled and sounded horrible, but that moment was the happiest I felt in a long time. Something about being on the 5 made me feel free. It had been what seemed like forever since I was headed to the beach with friends – jamming to music, laughing, and just hanging out. After many weeks spent begging for change and sitting on the cold, wet sidewalk, heading out of town felt freeing.

*My sorrow. Mi libertad.*

It seemed like no time had passed before we were in Edmonds. Mike steered into the parking lot next to the dog park. We piled out of the van and ran down to the beach. It was drizzling a lit bit, but that sure as hell wasn't going to stop us from our beach time. None of us had been out of the city in a long-long time. We found a giant piece of gnarled driftwood to use as a bench. Elisa was so excited she was literally jumping up and down. She then decided she was going to try to make a "sand angel." Her black lace-up boots, ginger braids, and clothes quickly filled with sand. It was a terrible idea – it was also hilarious.

Joe and Mike found an old soggy tennis ball that probably escaped the dog park. They were running up and down the beach, throwing it around. They had huge smiles on their faces, and I could hear them laughing as they played. They laughed even harder when they fell after tripping in holes or over logs. I wondered what they were like as little boys. Did they ever have the chance to frolic worry-free?

I slowly walked away from my friends towards the sound. I paused to appreciate the beauty of the snow-capped Olympic Mountains. I rocked my feet back and forth to push my boots further into the soft sand. I was grounding myself – strong like a warrior. I opened my arms to the sky. The wind filled my jacket and blew my wild hair straight out behind me. I closed my eyes; the salty mist from the waves kissed my face. I took deep breaths and let the smell of salt and dead fish soften me. For the first time in months, I felt like I could take complete breaths. My shoulders slide down away from my ears, and I unclenched my teeth. Without the rumble of the city, I felt safe.

We stayed until we were hungry, cold, and drenched; the drizzle had turned into steady spitting droplets and back to a drizzle many times in the hours we played on the beach. It was almost dark, but we couldn't bring ourselves to head back to the city and our tents. I seriously could not remember when I had such a great day. Watching the waves roll in and listening to my friends laugh soothed my weary soul.

# X

# BROKEN

A FEW WEEKS later, while walking to the Ave to try to get some money, the rain started coming down harder than usual. Elisa, Joe, and I started running for cover. My foot slid out from under me. I started cracking up as did my friends; I was spread eagle on the ground. The rain pummeled me. My friends tried to pull me up. As I put pressure on my leg, I crumbled to the ground.

"*¡A la verga!* I cannot stand up," I yelped. The initial shock wore off, and my ankle was screaming. "It hurts so *pinche* bad."

My mom warned me a million times about the metal grates being slippery in the rain. I tried again to stand. I couldn't move my ankle at all! My friends dragged me under an awning.

"Should I call 911?" A young college age woman said as she approached us.

I searched my friend's faces for an answer – while they did the same. I hadn't noticed that I was groaning from the pain. I tried to speak but couldn't get it together to make actual words. Everyone was talking over each other.

"We don't have a car and I don't think she can get on a bus," Elisa said.

A crowd started to gather. I think I might have passed out. The next thing I remember, was being surrounded by bicycle cops.

"An ambulance is on its way."

This situation is going to be bad ... very bad; I thought. I heard the sirens and knew the ambulance was close.

"Do you have insurance? How can we contact your parents?" The paramedic asked.

There was no way around telling them the truth. They wouldn't let any of my friends go with me in the ambulance. They took me to the hospital where people go with no insurance. It was dirty and crowded. Every chair was full and some people who looked really ragged were sleeping on the floor.

"It really hurts. Please stop the pain," I begged.

They looked at me like they do all street kids – like I was just trying to get drugs.

"Damnit! It hurts. Help me!"

"Here is some ibuprofen, it should take the edge off," the tired looking nurse said.

"*Cabrona*, are you kidding me? That is not going to stop the pain."

"That's all I can give you until after we get some x-rays, sorry."

It took a few more hours before anyone came to wheel me down for the x-rays. While waiting, I was lined up on a hospital bed in the hall with as many other patients as they could cram in. I heard screams and crying. I wanted my mom more than you can imagine. Relief came, after shift change. My new nurse pulled out the pain chart with the smiley to frowny faces.

"On a scale from one to ten, how bad is the pain?" Her eyes and hair were the same color of bluish grey. She had a thick accent; from I do not know where.

"Like twelve," I responded.

"Let me give you something a little stronger and maybe you can get some sleep, sweetie."

Finally, I thought. That nurse was gentle and kind. She came across like someone's grandma. I liked her immediately. She sat next to me, instead of standing over me when she talked to me.

"Sweetie, I have to call social services."

"I know." She touched my shoulder gently.

"I'll come back soon and check on you. Ok? Just shout if you need me."

Fortunately, I didn't break anything. I had a major sprain and would need to use crutches for six to eight weeks. I conceded that being on the street would be brutal under these conditions.

The social worker didn't arrive until after midnight. She drove me to another home that took emergency cases.

"Your previous caseworker is no longer with the agency. Your case has been assigned to Sara, but she doesn't work at night. She will get in touch with you tomorrow. She's nice. I think you'll like her."

"Sounds great," I said with more than a hint of snark.

On the way to the next house, I secretly hoped I'd go back to the perky lady's house. I was exhausted from the long day, hours waiting, and the meds. It would be nice to wake up to waffles, bacon and those cute kids.

As we turned south on I-5, I realized we weren't headed to Becky's. Instead, I ended up at the home of a very old and very grumpy lady. She told me almost immediately and repeatedly, "I have fostered over 38 teens, in my years doing this work." I wasn't sure how I was supposed to respond, so I said nothing.

"I should have retired decades ago," she added.

I agreed, but was smart enough to not share that thought with her.

# XI

# SOMETHING DIFFERENT

SARA, MY NEW social worker, seemed different from the minute I met her. She called Barb, the grumpy lady, before coming over and asked her if we'd like coffee, she was stopping for some on her way over. I hadn't had a mocha in weeks, and I jumped at the offer. Well, not literally since I was on crutches. When Sara arrived, she chatted with Barb and me as we drank our coffee. Sara had long brown hair that went almost to her waist. She wore jeans, tucked into black boots, a red sweater and a huge bronze necklace with a piece of black stone in the middle.

"Barb, would you please leave us alone for a bit so I can chat with Delores?" Sara said after about fifteen minutes of us all sitting in the living room.

"Sure, no problem. I will be in the den if you need anything."

"Do you understand this placement was temporary?" Sara started her line of questioning, once we were alone.

"Yup, and I am thankful for that," I said. Sara laughed.

"Barb might not be the easiest to get along with, but her heart is in the right place. Do you have thoughts about where you'd like to go next?"

"You know about my mom's situation, right?"

"Only what is in the case notes. She's living in one of the tent cities, right?"

"Well yeah, for now. She is struggling. It isn't her fault. She just had a series of bad things happen and kinda spiraled down."

Sara listened intently as I explained my mom's situation. She didn't jump in, cut me off, or thrust solutions at me. She just listened.

"Is there anything you can do to help her?" I asked hopefully.

"I can't promise any quick magic solution to make everything better. I can, however, promise I will do my best. My first priority is to make sure you are safe. Then, we can see what options are available to help your mom. Ok?"

"I really hate the group homes. That's why I ran away. There are too many girls in them. And I felt like I was in prison. There's no privacy and no respect. Please, don't make me go back there."

"I'm sorry those experiences were so horrible for you. Unfortunately, we have no open spaces for teens in foster homes, right now. However, you do have a couple of group homes you can choose from. There is one open on the south side of town and another on the north end."

"So, you are going to let me decide which one I want to go to?"

"Yes. Here, I brought the rules of both houses to show you. Other teens have told me the rules are one thing they really hate about the group homes, so I thought maybe if you could check them out beforehand, you'd kind of know what you were getting in to."

"How many girls are in each house? What about school? I don't want to go back to that horrible school I was in before."

We talked about the options for at least an hour. Even though it still felt like I was choosing the lesser of two evils, I was glad that I had a choice. It was nice to feel heard. At the end of the conversation, I decided to go to the home in the south end. I know the area better and thought I would be more comfortable there. Also, when I earned bus pass privileges again, I already knew the busses and would be able to get around easily on my own.

"Promise though, that you'll get me out of the group home as soon as you can?"

"I'll do my best, that I can promise."

"Fair enough," I said.

I guess I knew it was unlikely that I would be able to be with my mom again any time soon. I also knew the street wasn't an option. I had to play by their rules for a bit. After I gave her my decision about the group home, Sara stayed a little longer. She genuinely seemed like she wanted to get to know me. She also didn't seem like she was in a hurry. It made me uneasy. Why was she so nice? And why was she acting like she cared what I thought? It made me like her and not trust her at the same time.

"I have to get to my next visit, but I'll make arrangements with Anita, the house mom, and will pick you up in the next couple of days. Get some rest. I told Barb that the hospital wants you to just rest for a few days. So, she will give you time to watch movies and hang out," Sara concluded.

"Thanks, I'm tired."

"Thank you for sharing your thoughts with me. I understand you'd prefer to be in a foster home instead of a group home. I'll see what I can do."

I was surprised when Sara called Barb the next morning, and said that I could move to the new home that afternoon.

When I got to the car, Sara handed me a mocha.

"Thank you, that was really nice."

"No problem. I know you like them. So, can I ask you a couple of questions?"

"Sure." Admittedly, my heart skipped a few beats. I didn't want to talk about my mom and the situation right now.

"I was just wondering what you are worried about most right now?"

"Mostly, my mom. I hate this situation but I'm ok. I really don't know if she is."

Talking to her was easy. Perhaps because it seemed like she was interested in what I had to say?

"There wasn't much about your dad in the file. Would you mind telling me a little more about him?"

"They deported him. I haven't been able to see him since. We used to have so much fun together. My mom and dad loved each a lot. He always brought her roses and sometimes, I'd catch them dancing in the living room. After he got taken from us, things went to shit."

Sara's eyes filled with tears.

"Thank you for sharing that. I cannot imagine how hard this has been."

"Thanks. I don't wanna talk anymore. Ok?"

"Sure. Do you want to listen to some music? I drive so much that I decided to get satellite radio. You can find any music you can imagine on there."

I started skipping through the stations and stopped when I heard *La Chona*. I have a soft spot for it, and since we were talking about my *papi*, Mexican music was exactly what I needed. We listened in silence for the rest of the drive. I stuck to the Mexican channel. The music fluctuated from lively to excruciatingly sad.

We pulled up in front of the group home. It was a long cream colored one story with a black roof. There was a small porch with a few potted plants and a hanging basket filled with flowers. Along the front of the house was a raised brick planter containing ferns and juniper shrubs. The house seemed like it was probably built in the 1950s. The neighborhood looked clean and empty. I did not see a single person in their yards or walking down the street.

"Do you want to finish this song before going in?" Sara asked.

"Yes, please." The song was *Volver, Volver*, by Vicente Fernández, one of my *papi*'s favorites.

When the song ended, Sara looked at me and said: "Ready?"

"As ready as I can be." Sara grabbed my backpack since I was still fumbling with the crutches. The house mom greeted us with a big smile. Her hair was in tiny braids stacked high on her head and held up by a colorful flowered scarf.

"One of the other girls moved rooms so you can have a bed downstairs."

"Thank you."

There were only six teen girls at this home; there were three bedrooms for the residents, so I only had to share with one person. Already, an improvement from the last group home. Sara and Anita showed me to my room and told me I had a dresser to myself and would share the closet. I had to laugh at this point; I only had the clothes in my back pack which amounted to one pair of jeans, two ripped T-shirts, a couple of pairs of socks and underwear.

"Thanks, I don't really have anything to put in a dresser or closet, though."

"I will make sure we get you some new clothes this week," Sara said.

"Ok, we can go over the house rules after dinner. Why don't you rest here for a bit? Most of the girls will be getting home from school in a moment. Once you hear chatter in the common room – please go introduce yourself. Your roommate is at her Independent Living Program (ILP), so you'll meet her later. She is seventeen and getting ready to age out this summer," Anita said. I was immediately envious since that meant she was almost free.

"Do you need anything else from me before I go?" asked Sara.

"No. But hey, thank you for being nice to me."

"Of course. You deserve nothing less." I looked away uncomfortably. "I'll call you tomorrow to check in, ok?" She added.

"Thanks," I said.

After Sara left, I plopped down on the bed. My ankle still hurt a ton and it made it hard to sleep, but also made me exhausted. I stared at the ceiling thinking about how to get in touch with Mike, Elisa, and Joe, and, of course, my mom. Always thinking about how to get in touch with my mom. I must've dosed off because I woke up to the sound of a mixture of laughter and arguing. The other girls must be home, I thought. Guess it's time to meet them.

I hobbled to the common room and caught my crutch on a basket filled with magazines and almost fell on my face. All the girls started laughing; I laughed too. Guess that was my icebreaker.

"Hi, I am Didi, I guess you know that I'm new here?"

"I also know you're kind of clumsy," one of the girls said giggling.

I looked at her blankly. Then she pointed to my wrapped-up ankle.

"Apparently," I responded. I never thought of myself as clumsy before, but considering my entrance to the room and my recent fall I would say her assessment was valid. She seemed like a real smart ass; I thought I liked her. As it turned out, she was my roommate.

## XII

# BUDDING FRIENDSHIP

THE RADIANT SMART ass, named Mona, quickly became my best friend. Mona had copious curly shoulder-length jet black hair and stunning hazel eyes lined with dazzling, long lashes. She often wore tight black dresses and crazy colorful tights that hugged her curvaceous body. She rarely wore make-up but when she did – it was bright red lipstick. Mona and I clicked. Being around her was easy for me. Within a few days, I felt like I could tell her anything and she wouldn't judge me. She also had a wicked sense of humor and made me laugh harder than I had since everything started falling apart with my family. She was one of those people that scares some off because of her intensity. She could be intimidating, but it didn't take me long to figure out how incredibly brilliant she was. There was no one else in the house that could come up with a comeback like Mona could. And the dry delivery of her humor was on point. Mona sometimes used a wheelchair to help her get around, which was why she was also in the downstairs bedroom. She'd been through a lot of shit but was determined to "do something with her life." One night when we were up late talking, she shared with me some intensely painful parts of her life story.

"I've been in foster care on and off pretty much my whole life. Well, I was adopted when I was six but they returned me when I was ten because I was having a lot of medical problems and they decided that it was too much. So, my adoptive parents, or should I say ex-parents, relinquished their rights and sent me back to foster care. I'm surprised you never asked the dreaded question, 'What is wrong with you?'"

"I won't lie. Of course, I was wondering why it's so hard for you to walk and why you need the wheelchair sometimes. I just thought it was rude to ask."

"I was born with cerebral palsy. My symptoms weren't bad when I was little. After the CP got worse and they gave me back, I bounced around between foster and group homes. I was even in an institution for a while when they couldn't find anyone that would take me in. Before moving in here, I was on the streets for a couple of months. I didn't want to give up school though. I rode the busses most nights and went to school in the morning. My teachers got mad at me if I fell asleep though, so sometimes, if I was too tired, I didn't go. And of course, a lot of the kids were assholes. They acted like because I used a wheelchair, I couldn't hear or something. They would say shit about me like I wasn't even there."

"That sucks, people are so *pinche* mean!"

"It's ok, really. I just told them to fuck off."

"Really, it didn't bother you?"

"Nope, I don't give a shit what they think. They don't know nothing about me or my life. Fuck them for judging me. I've been in over twenty schools, none of those people will remember me. Before I got here, I was only in a school for like a minute. Who knows? It could be that they decide to move me from here too. After bouncing around, I realized I am the only person who can look out for me. I have to take care of myself. I thought about it a lot and I really want to help other kids like us. The only way I can do that is to go to college. Nothing is gonna stop me. I also want to make enough money to help my sister and nieces and nephews. They live in Alabama and things are bad down there. There's no jobs and people are even more racist than up here," Mona asserted.

"That's heavy, Mona."

"It is what it is. I'm not going to let all the drama keep me from being happy and doing what I want with my life."

"¡Órale, Mona! I feel lost compared to you. I don't even know what I'm doing tomorrow."

"You might want to start thinking about what you want. Seriously. You gotta learn to use this system. You're stuck in it. Use it to your advantage and keep your eye on getting the hell out of it. But, don't let it destroy you."

She stated all of this calmly like it was just a matter of fact. She didn't seem pissed off or anything. I couldn't tell if she was just fronting or simply resigned to the situation.

"It's different for me though," I said. "My mom and I will be back together someday." "Ok," she said. "I know you need to believe that."

"What is that supposed to mean?" I said angrily.

"Nothing, I hope your mom gets clean and things work out. Let's get some sleep." Mona replied.

I laid in bed staring at the ceiling. In my heart, I knew that Mona was right. I had to start thinking about what I would do if my mom couldn't get it together. But I couldn't do it yet. One day at a time was all I could do. I was conflicted and torn up about everything. I'm was angry at my mom – just for being my mom. And angry at her for not acting like a mom. And angry at the state, and my case workers and all the people who were trying to support me because they were also the ones keeping me from my mom.

# XIII

# ADJUSTING

Mornings at Anita's house were organized chaos. Anita must have drunk a lot of coffee before we got up because she was perpetually ready to solve whatever crisis one of the girls threw at her. Her makeup was subtle and effortlessly perfect. She loved wigs, so I never knew what look she'd be going with from one day to another. She often wore colorful scarves and flowy skirts. Anita reminded me of a classy jazz singer. Maybe it was because sometimes I could hear her singing before we all got to the kitchen. She had a remarkable voice, and Billie Holiday's songs seemed to roll effortlessly from her lips, filling the empty room with beauty while she cooked.

Although Anita was different in a lot of ways from the other house moms, we still didn't have any say about what we ate. Breakfast generally reminded me of the continental breakfast we had at cheap hotels, back before my *papi* got deported. He loved driving over to the coast and watching the storms roll in. In fact, I don't think we ever went to the coast in the summer. I always thought it was weird that, being from México, my *papi* loved stormy rainy cold days. He said the storms on the coast weren't as dramatic as those in Michoacán. He missed the thunder and lightning, which happened almost every night in the summer in his *pueblo*. Anyway, back to my point. Breakfast at Anita's kind of sucked. Options included doughy pre-packaged plain bagels, hard boiled eggs,

61

yogurt, bananas, and various bland types of cereal. However, Anita insisted that each of us "ate something."

Looking back, she handled a house full of teens amazingly well. Getting six of us to four different schools couldn't have been an easy task. Two girls went to the neighborhood public high school, two had taxi vouchers to go across town to their old high schools, and my smarty pants roommate went to community college. Anita recommended, to my social worker, that I go to the alternative high school to make up credits because I missed a ton of school in the last couple years. I was super reluctant because I always heard that those were schools for the bad kids and that gangs hung out around there. I knew I had been in some trouble but I didn't think of myself as one of the tough kids. The only other option was the neighborhood high school with the other girls, but that was my old school and I still hadn't figured out who turned me into CPS. I did NOT want to go back there. I reluctantly agreed the alternative school was the best option.

My first day at the new school, Anita drove me to meet with the principal. The building looked like it was a repurposed elementary school. It was a one-story long brick building with huge windows and a big playground. We parked in the back and entered through the double doors. The hallway was filled with posters and I could hear the buzz of the florescent lights. Everything was painted white and the floors were school house white tile with black flecks. Student artwork was hung everywhere and I could see a spray-painted graffiti wall at the end of the hall. A door suddenly opened and a middle-aged woman with a bleached blonde bouncy short bob, an enormous cup of hot cup of coffee in one hand, and a giant stack of papers in the other nearly bumped into us.

"Hi, Can I help you find someone?"

"We're here to meet the principal," Anita said.

"Great! That's me. I'm Claudia. I was expecting you. Didi and Anita, right?"

"Correct," Anita responded. I was not eager to talk.

"Follow me. I'm really glad you decided to go to school here, Didi," Claudia chirped. I resisted the temptation to tell her that I didn't have much of a choice.

Every windowless wall in her office contained bookshelves stuffed with binders, textbooks, and colored copy paper. Her desk was covered in papers and manila folders, there was barely enough room for her to set her coffee down. There was an open Chinese take-out container. I wondered if it was yesterday's lunch or breakfast? As soon as we sat down in her office, the questions started.

"What are your goals? What are your strengths? What are your challenges? Why did you stop going to school before?"

My mind started racing, too many thoughts at once, and then I blanked out. Why does everyone ask me so many questions? Answering their questions over and over again, is so exhausting. I just wanted to sleep. I just want to go home, wherever that is. I completely checked out during the meeting. I kept thinking about my mom. I responded only when prodded. Honestly, I'm not even sure what I said. The end result was they needed to get my records from my previous school, and I could take some placement tests the next day.

"Ok," I said. "Are we done?"

"For now," Claudia replied. Then she added, "Seattle Alternative School can be really good for you. If you try, you can make up your credits quickly and be back on track to graduate in no time."

"Ok," I responded.

"Didi, please give it a chance," Anita said flashing me her warm smile.

As Anita drove us back to the house, she asked "Are you ok?" I gave her a sideways glance.

"Stupid question," she said. "I know this is hard for you. You worried about your mom?" Again, I shot her a sideways glance. "Another stupid question, sorry. Would you like to check your Facebook when we get home to see if she messaged?"

"Of course," I said and after too long of a pause added "Thank you."

I knew she didn't have to allow me to use social media yet. When we got back to the house, I hobbled as quickly as possible to the computer. I hurriedly logged on to Facebook. Anita didn't ask me for my password, I think she conveniently forgot. The house rules said all passwords must be available to the house mom (in other words Anita). She stayed in the room while I was online, but pretended to be busy sorting books on the bookshelf on the other side of the room.

As soon as I logged in, I saw I had six messages. Several were from Mike, Joe, and Elisa asking me how my ankle was doing and where I was and one was from Tina. I didn't click on it though, because I didn't want her to know I saw it. I hadn't seen her since I left and didn't know what to say. My heart raced, there was a message from my mom.

"Didi, the social worker told me what happened. I'm so sorry you got hurt. I wish we could be together. I want to make you soup and curl up under a blanket and watch movies together. I miss you so much. The social worker said we can see each other if it's at her office. Do you want to do that? It's totally weird but at least we can see each other, right? I talked to her to see if she could help me get on disability because of my back. She said that there must be some job I could do and that I need to try harder. I'll try. I promise. I filled out two applications last week. I'm also on the waiting list for a women's treatment center. The wait right now is a couple of months. I miss you. I love you. – Mommy"

Tears ran down my face as I read the message. I took a big breath and logged off. I couldn't respond.

Anita walked over to me and put her hand gently on my shoulder.

"You've had a long day, why don't you go rest and get off that leg."

"Thank you," I mumbled as I grabbed my crutches.

# XIV

# ATYPICAL SCHOOL

Mona woke me up by plopping her backpack down on my bed. I must have fallen asleep almost immediately when my head hit the pillow.

"Hey lady, how'd it go at SAC?"

"What? What time is it?" One of the tricky parts of winter napping, is that if you take an afternoon nap you often wake up to darkness. It could be 5pm or 11pm, who knows?

"It's 5:30, I just got home and dinner's almost ready."

"Ok, I'm getting up" I said.

Groggily, I made my way to the dining room. I could not wait to get off the damn crutches. My stomach started rumbling as soon as I smelled the garlic bread. Everyone else was already gathered around the table. Since I was still waking up the chatter overloaded my senses. I knew I had to be quick though, whoever ate the fastest got seconds. If I was too slow or didn't take all that I needed the first helping, I'd be out of luck. Anita always made the biggest pot of spaghetti imaginable. However, many of the girls didn't have enough food growing up and were not shy about digging in. Dinner time frequently felt like a competition. Everyone would reach right across your plate to grab what they wanted. And those girls were moving fast. Anita often had to referee.

"Hey y'all, you don't need to take six pieces of bread. How about a little salad on those plates instead of a mountain of spaghetti? Make sure everyone gets some."

"C'mon I'm hungry. Hurry up. Pass that pasta. I didn't eat lunch at school. It looked like dog shit," said Tammi, an extremely tall athletic girl with short braids and gorgeous mocha colored skin.

Besides Mona, I don't know much about the other girls. I tended to keep to myself when we were in the common rooms and often tuned everyone out. I also avoided being in the group whenever possible. Mona and I talked when we were alone. We were allowed to be in our room more than the others because Anita knew Mona was serious about school. Mona would always say she was going to study, Anita believed her. I got to tag along by saying I was going to read. Anita kept lots of books in the common room trying to encourage us to read. So, saying you were reading was a free pass to get out of spending time in the common room. Mona was incredibly intelligent. She didn't need that much time to study, therefore we had a lot of time to chat in the evenings.

A huge whiteboard in the kitchen listed the chores for each resident for the week. Mona and I were off the hook from kitchen duty that night. After dinner, we went straight back to our room.

"You never did tell me about how it went at SAC," Mona said.

"I had to answer all the same questions over and over again. Now they are making me take tests to see where I'm at with math and stuff. I'm totally dreading it." I know I sounded whiny, but I was frustrated.

"This is your chance to catch up. That school really helps kids out. I know other people that went there and the teachers really seem to care," Mona said.

"God Mona, you sound like you should work there! Lay off, ok."

"I'm just trying to help. You're so emo sometimes."

"¡Chingao!" I said. Then we started laughing.

Deep down, I knew she was trying to help. But it was hard to put any effort into anything. I had no hope. I felt like I needed to get through each day, but I couldn't think about anything beyond that. I wasn't a very social person like a lot of kids are. I hated being in foster care. I didn't want to make new friends. I hated being in another new school and catching up with my credits seemed like an impossibility.

"Guess I better get try to get some sleep. I hear you test better that way," I said sarcastically.

"Yeah, I've heard something like that too," Mona replied laughing.

The next morning, Anita greeted me with a huge blueberry muffin, a bag of nuts, and a big glass of orange juice.

"It's good to be well fed before testing." Anita said. She was wearing her short curly wig with light brown highlights. I loved that one, the curls bounced when she moved her head or laughed enthusiastically.

"Thanks, Anita."

After the other girls got out the door for school, Anita drove me back to SAC. She tried her best to encourage me on the way.

"You're gonna do great. Don't worry too much. Just do your best. This isn't high stakes testing. They're designed to help the school figure out which classes you should be in and what you already know." Then she broke out into song, as she often did.

> *Although we know there's much to fear*
> *We were moving mountains*
> *Long before we knew we could, whoa, yes*
> *There can be miracles*
> *When you believe...*

The school wasn't far from the house, I probably could have walked if I wasn't on crutches. We pulled into the parking lot and Anita stopped singing.

"You really should sing professionally. You're amazing. What's the name of that song?"

"It's 'When you Believe' by Whitney Houston. I believe in you, Didi."

"Thanks, Anita. Glad somebody does. No need to walk me in. I got this," I said, even though I didn't believe it.

I grabbed my backpack and crutches and carefully navigated the cracked sidewalk. It was raining and the last thing I wanted was to fall again. My crutches squeaked on the tile as I lumbered towards Claudia's office.

"Hey. Good morning, Didi. We still don't have your school records, but the tests will help us see what you know so far. Just do your best," Claudia said.

"Sounds great." I said, trying to channel Anita's positivity. I doubt I was convincing.

I was super distracted while I took the tests, I still hadn't written my mom back. All I could think about was when I would see her, if she was ok, and if we would ever get to live together again. My ankle also hurt like hell. I didn't sleep good the night before because of my long afternoon nap, and honestly I couldn't force myself to care about the tests at all.

It was also awkward because the only place for me to take the tests was in Claudia's office. She answered phone calls, people came in to ask her questions all while I was supposed to be "doing my best" on algebra and reading comprehension tests. The testing took a couple of hours and then Claudia offered me a sandwich and chips for lunch. After I finished, she said that she'd like me to speak to the school counselor for a bit. Fantástico, I thought. Another counselor. I had an appointment scheduled later that same week to talk to a psychologist, plus a meeting with my social worker, Sara, to "check in", and I also had to go back to the doctor so he could check my ankle. It often felt like all I did was go to meetings. AND all of them ask the same questions, over and over again. If only they would actually talk to each other instead of grilling me.

Claudia walked me down to the counselor's office. My crutches were dry now – at least my squeaking didn't attract unwanted attention from every student in the building. Francis, the counselor, had his door slightly open and was typing away on his computer. He stood up to greet us. He was tall, lanky and a little too skinny for his height. He had short styled dirty blonde hair, and extremely green eyes that I would have suspected were contacts, except he was rearing black 50s style glasses. I immediately pegged him as a hipster "wanna be", but he was a little too nerdy to pull it off. To complete his look, he had on black skinny jeans, a black T-shirt, and a vest like a fancy man would wear under a suit jack. After our introduction, Claudia told Francis to walk me back to her office when we were done talking.

"No hurry," Claudia said, "Take all the time you want." Great I thought.

Francis pointed to a two-cushioned plaid sofa against the wall.

"Feel free to help yourself to snacks any time you want. There's a basket of chips, some fruit over there, and juice boxes in the frig. Would you feel comfortable if I shut the door while we talk?"

"Sure?" I said.

"Things are a little different here at SAC. I meet with every student at least every other week. My door is open to everyone here at the school. The teachers often come when they want to talk about something, vent whatever. Claudia even comes to talk with me."

"Interesting" I said. Not really sure why I said it.

"So, I just want you to know you can talk to me anytime. I won't share with anyone else the things we talk about – unless of course you tell me that you are a thinking of harming yourself or someone else. Understand?"

"Sure," I said.

"I'd like for us to learn about each other. Would you like me to start or do you want to?" Francis said.

"Go ahead," I said reluctantly.

I had sat in numerous offices talking to a multitude of people since I went into care. I was definitely not interested in learning about Francis or telling him about my life. He didn't seem to care. He launched into telling me about his brothers and sisters and growing up in Salt Lake City, adding he is not Mormon. Funny, how people that grow up in Salt Lake feel the need to tell you immediately where they or their family falls on that one. As he talked, I looked around his office at the wall of books and pictures of people rock climbing. I assumed he was one of the climbers.

"Ever since I was a child, I knew I wanted to help people. I absolutely love my job. I totally lucked out, this is my first job since graduating and it's awesome. I think I'll stay here for a long time. And Seattle is rad. I am so stocked to be living here." What a dork I thought.

"Ok, your turn."

"Don't you already know?" I asked.

"Claudia told me you were in a group home, but I don't know anything else."

"Well, besides being in a group home and having this messed up ankle there isn't really much more happening."

"Do you want to talk about your parents?"

"Nope."

"Can you tell me a little about what you hope to achieve while you are SAC?"

"Being done with it," I replied. Perhaps a little too honestly.

"Delores, it seems like you don't feel like talking today. Am I right?"

"Yup."

"We can hang out and listen to music instead if you wanna?" Francis then turned his computer monitor to me and showed me his playlists. He told me to choose anything I wanted.

"Thanks," and then I added, "I go by Didi."

Then I clicked on "Praying" by Kesha and we listened for a while in silence. At the end of the song Francis started asking me questions about what I liked about that song.

"It feels like she understands."

"Yeah, I feel the same way about a lot of the musicians I listen to."

"You really like music too, don't you?"

"Love it. Makes everything better."

"Yeah, and sometimes it makes me cry when I feel like I need to but can't. You know?"

"Yeah, I do."

We spent the rest of the afternoon chatting about music. I was kind of surprised about how much he knew about music, not only from the US but some of the classic Mexican music my *papi* loved as well. We took turns playing songs for each other. I couldn't believe when he played Chavela Vargas. She was one of my *papi's* other favorites. He used to say that her voice made your heart feel every word she sang.

"Wow, school is almost out for the day. I better walk you down to Claudia's office. Will you come by my office later this week?"

"Sure," I again replied. But I actually meant it. I hated to admit it but he seemed kind of nice.

# XV

# FENTANYL

"DIDI, WAKE UP." I opened my eyes and Anita was standing next to the bed. I immediately knew something terrible happened. We were all responsible for getting ourselves up, she never came into the room to get us up.

"It's my mom, right?"

"She's ok. But she is in the hospital. I called Sara and she is out of town, so another social worker will give you are ride to the hospital. I'm sorry, I can't take you but you know...I have to get the other girls off to school."

I jumped out of bed and put on the first things I could grab from the closet. Mona woke up when I was talking to Anita. She gave me a huge bear hug before I left. Few words were spoken.

We got to the notorious hospital, that people without insurance go to, as the sun was rising. It is also a trauma hospital, which means people who have experienced the most horrible things often end up there. We circled the parking lot a few times to find an empty space. I almost jumped out of the moving car. I couldn't sit still, I needed to see my mom. As we entered through the emergency doors, chaos greeted us. It felt dirty for a hospital. The waiting room was packed. People crying, coughing, and looking empty and hopeless. A man sat attached to an IV pole, he had a long metal rod sticking out of his leg. Sirens wailed as an ambulance arrived. The social worker, John, walked me to the nurse's station. He told them who we were and asked if I could see my mom. The nurse seemed bothered by our existence. In a town with an opioid crisis, you'd think people would be filled with compassion. Instead, they generally seemed annoyed by having to deal with another life in decay.

When we came around the corner I could see into my mom's room. She was sleeping. Even from the distance, I could tell she looked like shit. I guess it is hard not to when you are strung out. I missed the old her. She was wearing the classic hospital gown and had those tubes that give you oxygen stuck in her nose. I was told later that a lot of times they send patients who OD home right away after they recover. There must have been some kind of complication. I was too upset to think about asking the nurses why she was still there.

On a chair next to the bed, was a slender woman in her thirties. She had dishwater blonde hair that was pulled back into a tight pony-tail on the top of her head. She was wearing a beige puffy coat, sparkly fuchsia leggings, and rain boots. Her intense umber eyes were tear stained. I had never seen her before. She looked up at me and our eyes met.

"I am so sorry. This shouldn't have happened. I'm Jen, I live down at the camp with your mom. She's one of the best friends I've ever had. You, Didi?"

"Yes. What the hell happened?"

Jen then painfully and tearfully relieved the experience as she explained how the OD happened.

'Officer's, please! Please. Please help! My friend…I can't wake her up'. I screamed at the bicycle cops I saw riding towards me.

'Where is she? Calm down! What happened?' A lot of people were talking at once. Everyone was freaking out.

'She's in the alley, right around the corner. Hurry, please. We didn't mean for it to happen. She was so sick. She just wanted to get better. It was only a little'.

I started running back towards your mom. The bicycle cops followed me. When I got to your mom, she was still crumpled into a pile by the dumpster. There was trash everywhere around her. The cops jumped off their bikes and leaned them against the brick wall. The alley smelled like a mixture of rain beer, and piss. It was so horrible.

'Call for medical back up.' The cop with a short goatee yelled to his partner. Then he looked at me and was like, 'You need to tell me what happened, right now, or I cannot help her.'

'Heroin', I whispered. I could hardly say it. I was panicking. Then I told them, 'She's been trying to get clean, she really wanted to stay clean. She was just so sick. Please help her.'

The goateed cop looked over his shoulder and yelled, 'Narcan' to the other cop. He was a beefy looking young dude.

'On it' his partner said.

He was opening the saddlebags on his bike. Then he pulled out a box wrapped in plastic. He still had his helmet on, when he crouched down by your mom and fumbled to open the over-dose kit. He handed something to the goateed cop as he prepared the plunger. Next, he put it into your mom's nose to give her the naloxone. It all happened really fast.

'Now we wait,' he said.

'Isn't there something else we can do?' I begged.

'Talk to her,' he said.

'I am so sick of this shit.' I heard the goateed cop mutter under his breath.

We sat staring at your mom for a couple of minutes waiting for something to happen. A rat scurried about under the dumpster. Then I heard sirens. I thought about running, but I couldn't leave her. We need each other. I have kids in the system too. Your mom and I are trying to kick so we can have our families back. We love our kids. She loves you. It seemed like it took forever until the ambulance pulled into the alley. It started raining hard, just then your mom made some noises and her eyes began to flutter.

As she told the story, tears slipped down my face. I placed my hand on my moms and she weakly grasped back. She eventually opened her eyes and said, "I'm sorry."

"Don't talk to me yet," I snapped. "I'm really mad at you." Then my silent tears turned to violent sobbing.

# XVI

# DIAGNOSE ME

THE NEXT COUPLE of days were filled with sorrow that I didn't think I would ever be able to exit. In those moments, I had no hope that my mom and I would be together again. It seemed like the junk had too strong of a hold on her and there was no way she could break free. I felt more alone than at any point in my life. I know that Mona and Anita tried everything they could think of to pull me out of my suffering, I didn't want to come out. Any moment that I wasn't forced into interaction, I hid in my room and curled up under the blankets. I wept and I stared at the ceiling. I was exhausted from the non-stop doctor check-ups, and appointments with my social worker, court appointed lawyer, and a psychiatrist.

After talking at me for about thirty minutes the psychiatrist diagnosed me with depression. I barely said anything to the old white dude, so I guess he determined I was depressed because I said nothing? He asked me to leave the room so he could talk to Anita. On the drive home, she told me the diagnosis and about the pills he recommended.

"Nope, not gonna happen. Anita, I'm not taking pills. I barely even talked to that old dude. What could he possibly know about what I need? Of course, I'm depressed. My life sucks."

"Didi, I can see you are upset. We need to talk this over with Sara. If she says you have to take the pills, then I am obligated to make you."

"Fine, call Sara. I'm not taking those pills."

"I'll call her when we get home."

We sat in tense silence the rest of the way home. Once again, I knew it was not Anita's fault but I was pissed off. The reason that my mom and I were in our situation was because doctors prescribed my mom a bunch of pills. Then they tried to force me to take pills. Wasn't it natural for me to seem depressed considering everything that had happened? I wanted them to put my family back together instead of giving my pills to make me stop caring.

The next bad news came when my school records made it to SAC. Apparently, I only had four credits out of the 24 needed to graduate. At the end of this semester, I should have had twelve. I was never in a special education class, but Claudia told me my previous school said I had a specific learning disability and oppositional defiance disorder (ODD). She asked me if I could tell her about accommodations and modifications that were helpful at my other schools.

"Well, I am guessing none since I only have four credits in almost two years?"

"Did anyone at the schools tell you how your disability affects your learning?"

"I do not have a disability. What the hell?"

"Sorry, I am just reporting what the records say."

"Can I talk to Francis about this instead of you?"

"Sure thing." And that was the end of that meeting, thankfully.

I was struggling. Luckily, I had Mona to calm me down. The best part of my day was at the end when Mona and I had time to talk alone. I told her about my new labels. And I cried through my rage. I wanted to break things and scream but I didn't want the other girls to see any weakness. I tried to play it tough and like I was in control. It's the whole idea of being in survival mode. If I was a victim, if I was seen as inferior – I would be eaten alive. I felt like I had to be stronger or at least appear to be stronger just to survive.

Later that week, Anita and I met with Sara. I explained to her that I didn't want to take the pills. Sara listened intently and seemed to really hear what I was saying.

"Anita, what do you think? How is Didi adjusting to your home and school?"

"Honestly, I see her shut down sometimes. But I also see her trying. I know she's super worried about her mom and that distracts her from school."

"Didi, do you have any thoughts of harming yourself?" Sara asked.

"Surprisingly, no."

"Why is that surprising?"

"Because my situation is pretty fucked. Yikes, sorry Anita." I added immediately, before Anita was even able to throw me the you messed up side glance.

"So, what motivates you now?" Sara added.

"I want to be with my mom. If I do anything to mess things up again that will make it less likely. I get that now. I am not going to hurt myself. Yes, I am depressed. I miss my family. I want to be with my dad too. We love each other. And it is horrible being apart." I then broke down and sobbed.

"I shouldn't go against the doctor, but I will approve that you don't have to take the medication for the next two weeks. Please don't make me regret this. I care about you and it could mean losing my job. Anita, please text me if anything changes and if you think Didi is not doing well."

"Really? Thank you so much. I will be ok. I just need to be sad sometimes. I am trying though. Mona won't let me not try."

"Yeah, Mona has it going on. I am glad you two have each other." Anita replied.

"Anything else I can help with?" Asked Sara.

"My mom. Have you heard from her? When can I see her?"

"We can work on setting up a supervised visit whenever you want. Anita, when would be best?"

"Could we do a Saturday or Sunday? Weekdays are so hard because of school and sports for all the girls."

"Absolutely. Didi, hopefully she will call soon and I will arrange it."

"She messaged me about meeting. Can I message her to tell her to call you?"

"Of course."

"Thanks."

That Friday, I finally got some good news. The doctor said my ankle was strong enough that I didn't need crutches anymore. Most of us take walking for granted. I ran into the house just because I could. When I went into the room and saw Mona's wheelchair, I stopped on a dime. I almost bragged about how I could walk and run again and how great it felt. I am so glad I didn't express those thoughts because Mona will never again experience those things. Mona spoke before I had a chance to say anything.

"No more crutches? Bet it feels great."

"It does, thank you! What are you up to?"

# XVII

# WHOSE LABELS?

M ONA CONTINUED TO be the voice of reason, which repeatedly offered a counter-narrative to what was in my head. I often resisted everyone that was trying to help me. I guess I was afraid of trusting anyone and had a hard time believing they actually cared about me. Mona always told me that it didn't matter if they cared or if they were just doing their jobs. She said that I needed to figure out how they could help me get where I wanted to go. And then, take the help they could give. That was hard. The last few years, taught me to take care of myself and not ask for help. But more and more, I realized I was pretty screwed and couldn't dig my way out alone.

When I went to meet with Francis, he tried to convince me there was hope.

"Don't panic. We can create a plan for you to earn credits quickly through credit retrieval programs."

Mona had told me about those, and said she took advantage of them and it was doable. Mona, being Mona also said she would help me. Seriously, where did she get her energy? And how did her heart remain so open after everything she had been through. Her laugh and smile had a way of radiating across a room and making everything seem just a little bit better. Although, I was of course super happy that she'd graduate and would be on her own at the end of the school year – I was already dreading her leaving me.

"Ok. My roommate told me the credit retrieval worked for her. I'll give it a try."

"Excellent. I have another appointment this afternoon. But come back tomorrow and we'll get to work."

"Ok."

A few night later when alone in our room, I shared with Mona the way the school had labeled me. I vaguely remembered all the tests and meetings with the school people. I was really pissed off about it, and I knew that I didn't try on those tests or tell them how I was feeling. I was careful about what I said because it was at a time when things were going badly for my mom. I guess I tried to protect her. I didn't want the school to know how bad shit was at home. I couldn't concentrate at all on school then. When I was little, I was always in the classes for the smart kids. I didn't think I had any problems learning. I just didn't care about school and couldn't concentrate.

"Most of the kids I met in foster care have some kind of label. At one point somebody put me down as 'borderline retarded' in my school records. As I bounced around from school to school, no one questioned it. They had me in the lower end of the special ed classrooms. They didn't really try to teach me much. It wasn't until I was in the seventh grade that Mrs. Jackson, my teacher, said, 'Why are you in this class?' She demanded they retest me. When the testing was over, they said I had dyslexia. It made sense after they explained what it meant. I wondered why I had such trouble reading. Now, I know I can use screen readers and audio books to help me learn. I wish it hadn't taken so long to know it. But it's ok. Now, I know," Mona shared.

"What? Wow? Weren't you super pissed off when you found out your label was wrong for all those years?" I was stunned.

"Maybe, but I wasn't shocked. I was supposed to see my social worker like every ninety days, and I hadn't seen her in over a year. It was almost like the system forgot about me."

It seemed every tragic experience I had, Mona had a story way worse than mine to tell. Yet, even while she told me about her horrible experiences, she laughed. Mona's determination was contagious. If she could handle everything she'd been through and graduate, I began to feel more like I could too.

"How do you handle the labels?"

"First use the support if it helps you, and if you don't need the help then fuck the labels. They are not you. Don't let them hold you back. Yeah. I think a lot of people label me too, but the only labels I recognize are ones that I actually give myself. Like, I am honest, smart and a hotty," she said while throwing her head back and laughing. "Seriously, nobody really knows a lot of things that are my essence. I say I'm an open person, but I really keep a lot of things close to chest because of my past and everything. Most people who are going to put a label on me probably put a negative label because it makes them feel better about themselves. I don't really subscribe to my labels unless they have a purpose and I adopt them as my own. Know what I mean?"

"Yeah, I guess. It's hard though. They sometimes make my heart hurt."

"I totally get that. You can do this though. Just keep going."

"Thanks, *amiga*."

If everyone had a friend like Mona, the world would be a better place. At previous group homes, I met girls who ran away, popped pills, and skipped school. They tried to get me to go along with them. This was the first time I had a roommate that was encouraging me to get my shit together and do better. She did it in a way that didn't piss me off either. I didn't feel like she was being bossy or implying she was better than me. I felt like she was encouraging me because she wanted me to be ok. I also lucked out being placed at Anita's.

The longer I stayed with her, the more my respect for her grew. Anita treated us all equally and continued to offer support even to the girls that were giving her the hardest time and after they seriously messed up. She was the best support system many of us had. Anita had to deal with girls running away and lashing out at her. While I was living with her, one girl, Sandra, got pregnant. Anita helped her find a doctor who would treat her with respect, went with her to talk with the social worker, and eventually helped her move to another home that was for teen moms. I'm not trying to stereotype girls in foster care, but I just think that when you are a teen girl, you go through a lot and experience a lot (whether you are in foster care or not). Everyone needs a good support system because you can break down a lot. I know I did. I am thankful for Anita's kindness and the love she gave to all of us.

At one of my other group homes, a girl named Missy was always trying to cut herself and overdosed on pills. She would cry and say she was so alone and had no one to talk with. I tried to be her friend, but she always got mad at me and told me not to tell her what to do. The foster mom at that home ran it like a business. None of us felt like we could open up about our lives and problems. That is why Anita was so unique. She maintained control of the house though and reminded us, "I am always here for you, but I am your parent for now, not your friend." She felt it was important to keep boundaries. During the time I was with Anita, I went through at least five social workers. Even the ones I liked didn't stay long before quitting or moving to a different office. I learned quickly to not confide in them since they wouldn't be staying long enough to help me anyway. When I had to meet with them, I would try to get through the questions as quickly as possible and get out. Anita and Mona were my lifelines.

# XVIII

# FROM THE DARKNESS

IT WAS MANDATORY for everyone in the house to come to the table for meals, but I could barely force food down my throat since my mom OD'd. Girls, in several of the group homes I was in before Anita's, mocked me for saying my mom would get clean and we would be back together soon. It made me so mad. I even threw a glass of water at one of the girls who said it. She just laughed and said, "you'll see." Unfortunately, a lot of the girls I met had family members who were addicted. It hardened them. While I still had the hope of being back with my mom, it was hard for me to dig in and focus on school or completely settle in at Anita's house. Before my mom OD'd, I firmly believed I wouldn't be in the system for too much longer. After, I was a zombie for months.

There was a lot of structure at Anita's house. We all had daily schedules that dictated when we got up, ate, did chores, homework, when we went to bed, and even designated time for "fun." There were planned activities we went to as a group to give us "positive social experiences." I complied. I no longer had the fight in me to resist. I got through each day by following the schedule and keeping my mouth shut. I noticed if I didn't say anything it was easier to stay numb. I could tell Mona was frustrated with me. She kept telling me to snap out of it and that I had to take care of myself. Other times Mona would come and sit next to me, not saying anything. She tried to hug me, but each time I let her I would break down and sob, so I stopped letting her.

And then a light flickered within the darkness. One morning I stepped outside and saw purple crocus pushing up through the ground in random spots in Anita's yard. They were disorganized (not in a flower bed). It was apparent they had been planted by squirrels. The air smelled sweet. I took a deep breath and looked up. The sky was blue with big fluffy clouds, instead of the one grey cloud that we usually had. I took another deep breath and looked around. The neighbor's cherry tree was starting to bloom. When did spring happen?

"Didi, C'mon. You are making us all late." Anita yelled. She and the others were already in the van.

"Sorry." I grabbed my backpack from the porch and ran to the van.

One of the girls turned on the radio and started singing along to Alicia Keys, "Girl on fire," and like usual the rest talked over each other. I didn't join in. However, that day I felt the seed of determination germinate. When I got to my first class, I asked the teacher if I could go talk to Francis.

"Sure," she said and handed me a hall pass.

I walked down the hall, which was lined with multi-colored lockers. There was a lot of really cool new student art on the walls, I hadn't noticed it had been changed. Was it always there or was it new? I wasn't sure, but it seemed there were many talented artists at SAC. As I got close to Francis's office, I heard the faint sounds of Pearl Jam's "Even Flow." His door was slightly ajar, I knocked lightly.

"Come in." Francis said cheerfully. As I entered his office, he put down his green smoothie.

"Hey, what's up? I haven't seen you in a while."

"Can you really help me?" I asked.

He spun in his chair, motioned to the sofa, and turned off the music in one sweeping move.

"I will certainly try my best to help," he responded.

We spent the next couple of hours talking. I couldn't believe how comfortable I felt telling him my life story. Francis never once looked at the time or acted like he had something else he should be doing. I felt like he was intently listening to what I wanted and that he wanted to help me succeed. We talked about how bouncing around put me so far behind and how frustrated I was with the social workers who always left. I told him that Sara seemed different and I hoped she wouldn't leave me. I even told him about how my mom OD'd. He was compassionate in his response, and I didn't feel like he was judging her or that he thought she was a horrible person. No matter what I said, he listened.

"Hey Francis, I think I talked enough today. Can we stop talking?"

"Of course, Didi. Thank you for sharing all this with me. I feel like I understand a little more about what you have been through and I have some ideas about how to help. Would you come back in a couple days so we can talk about getting you back on track with school? I understand earning money so you can see your dad is a high priority, we can talk about job options for when you turn 16. Before you go, can I ask you to try something new?

"Ok," I said a bit nervously.

"I'd like you to spend some time daydreaming. Allow yourself to dream of the life you want. I know it sounds cheesy. But it can be beneficial to give yourself permission to create in your mind the life of your dreams. What does your house look like? What color is it? Who are the people around you the most? Do you have a dog or cat? When you go to work, where do you go? What does your workspace look like? What makes you feel great? Will you please try it?"

"Yeah. Ok, I'll try it. And yes, it sounds incredibly cheesy. See ya later" I headed back to class still laughing. I didn't believe that visualizing the perfect life would make anything better. My mom and I used to make fun of people that talked like that, but I knew I wanted… needed… to do something different. If I wanted to get to my *papi*, I was going to have to figure out how to pull it together and earn a bunch of money before I turned 18. No one could do this for me.

That night during my computer time, I searched for pictures of Pátzcuaro, the *pueblo* where my *papi* lives. I tried to imagine myself being there and walking through the streets with him. All the buildings in el centro are painted the same. The bottoms are deep reddish-brown and the tops are cream colored. It's weird because the buildings look a lot like the ones in that movie that I watched with the perky lady's kids when I first got taken by CPS. I didn't even realize that then. There were moments when I could see myself there. Then the words I had been told so many times would creep into my head: "you can't afford to go to México. Kids like you don't leave here. You'll be lucky if you can find a job and make enough money to survive." I tried to stop the thoughts and go back to feeling myself in México. It didn't work. I was flooded with doubt. Who was I kidding? Will I ever be happy? I logged off the computer and asked Anita if I could to go to my room. I flung myself on the bed and stared at the ceiling until I fell asleep. I didn't even hear Mona come in that night.

For the next few Fridays, I met with Francis, and we worked on creating my transition plan (as he called it). He helped me download and print out pictures of Pátzcuaro. I was able to get my tía to send me a picture of my *papi*. Francis and I listened to music, and he helped me create a collage depicting my dream life. The more I worked on the collage, the more my dream felt possible. I could almost see myself sitting in the plaza next to my *papi*. I started to smell the flowers and *elote* roasting. Francis also gave me tips on how to stop all the negative thoughts in my head that tried to convince me it couldn't be done.

"Sometimes it helps me to just think the word 'Stop' when negative thoughts pop up in my head. I've learned that by doing that it stops the river of negativity from taking over my brain. Try not to beat yourself up. Just simply say 'Stop' and then try to go back to what you are trying to accomplish or the good thoughts you were having," Francis explained.

"Yeah, I'll try it. But I don't know if I can stop them. I get really excited about going to see my *papi*, but then I feel like I won't be able to pull it off. I mean, I am not even close to graduating, and I always seem to do something stupid or destructive just when things or going good and..."

"Stop."

"Huh?"

"See how I disrupted those negative thoughts by saying stop?"

"Yeah, but it's different cuz you distracted me."

"That's the point. It takes practice but over time you can learn to distract yourself from those negative thoughts. You can use any word you want, I just found 'Stop' works for me."

"Hmmm. Interesting. I'll think about it." I replied honestly. It did seem to help in that moment, I wondered if I could teach myself to do it.

When I think back, I am surprised how during those weeks Francis didn't even talk to me about grades or the classes I was in or should be taking. After I felt like the collage was done, Francis said it was time to back up and create a roadmap of how to make my dream become a reality. Then he helped me figure out how to catch up on my credits and start thinking about what kind of classes I was interested in. I worried a lot about getting a job to make money, but he promised we'd get to that when I was closer to 16. I couldn't legally work right now, so Francis encouraged me to use the time to catch up. Since SAC was an alternative school, there was more flexibility in what I was allowed to learn. I could do online classes, individual projects, or participate in group classes. We talked a lot about my previous experiences at school.

"Tell me about what classes you like the most and which ones you disliked. Then tell me why."

"A lot of the times it depended on the teacher. Sometimes, I like math. Other times it was social studies or language arts. It depended on how the teacher treated us kids. And if they actually seemed to like their job. You know what I mean? If the teacher seemed like they didn't want to be there, it was hard to want to be there. Like in my last school, there was a history teacher that seemed to hate all of us. She was continually accusing the African and Mexican kids of 'being disruptive'. They didn't talk more than any of the other kids, particularly since some of them barely spoke English. Finally, I got so sick of it I asked her, 'Why are you here? I have to be here. You get paid to be here. Even though it's a little, you still get paid. I have to be. So, if you don't want to be here, get the fuck out.' Needless to say, I got kicked out of that class. I told the principal that I was being honest. That didn't go over too well."

I have a tendency to be too blunt for most people. My mom always encouraged me to say what I thought and felt. Maybe, I did take it a little too far sometimes.

"I can see how frustrating it would be to have a teacher like that. It sounds like you're interested in a lot of things, though," Francis said.

"Totally, I know it sounds dorky but I like history and science too. I also like learning about different people and how things work in the world. And, I love art. I'm not good at making it myself, but I enjoy looking at what other people create."

"Have you heard about Chicano or Ethnic studies," he asked.

"Nope," I said.

"We can create your whole educational plan around a curriculum that is culturally relevant," Francis added.

Sometimes he threw around words and jargon that so fit the stereotype of an over-educated white dude, but the more I got to know him the more it made me see he actually cared and wanted to make life better for kids, like me, who were struggling. His enthusiasm for life and helping us was as contagious as Mona's. How did I get so lucky? I finally stopped resisting and jumped on the enthusiasm wagon too. I started to believe that I could catch up and I could get to my *papi*.

A bizarre thing happened; next, there were teachers who got excited when I got excited. They were like, "Yes! Finally! Okay! This is it! Oh my god! Hurray. Pinch me? Am I dreaming? Yeah, let's do this!" These teachers were ready to help me, and it built my confidence that I could make my dream happen.

After maybe a month or so of meeting with Francis for a few hours each Friday, I had a cool visual map of getting from where I was to where I wanted to be. He made me take a picture of it on my phone, and he laminated it for me to put up in my room. I felt kind of embarrassed, but I told Mona that Francis wanted me to hang it up.

"Let me see it." Mona shouted while almost grabbing it from my hands. "This is so cool. Your dad is cute. Wow! México has pine trees like we do? It's beautiful."

Mona was always a relentlessly enthusiastic cheerleader, of course. She seemed more excited than Francis or maybe even me about the collage.

"I'm totally gonna come visit you and your dad in México, and I am not even joking!" Mona gushed.

I believed her. Mona seemed to be able to do anything she put her mind too. I wanted to be like her. She encouraged me to look at the collage every day before heading out of the room – to keep my focus on the dream. I admit seeing my *papi*'s smile on that poster every day helped keep me going when I didn't feel like I wanted to.

Before I left for school, I had a few minutes to check my messages to see if there was any news from my mom. No new messages, so I decided to read the old ones.

"*Papi*, I decided I'm going to graduate and then I am going to be with you. You can't come here, but I can come to you! *Te amo, papi.*"

"*¡Mija, estoy tan feliz! Ya estoy aquí, esperándote.*"

Going to México was the only way for us to be together since he couldn't come back to the US. It was far too dangerous for him to try to cross because of all the craziness that was happening at the border. We'd been apart for over five years. It hurts to think it would be another couple of years before we could be together again. But I finally felt like it was possible. My *papi* said, once I got there, he could help me get residency (or even citizenship) and I could stay. He also started telling me about colleges near his town. I had to ask him to hold up. "Let me get through High School first!" I didn't know if I even wanted to go to college.

As I got more focused on school, Anita started easing up on restrictions around using the computer and told Sara she thought it would be ok for me to have a cell phone again. It took a few months, but I finally convinced Anita and Sara that I wasn't a runaway risk. Then, I was given a bus card and a cell phone. It wasn't anything fancy, but at least I had a phone again and could use Facebook to talk to my parents. The rule was that Anita had to have the passwords for all my accounts.

I knew it made her feel as uncomfortable as it did me, but I understood. Some of the girls that lived with us had been involved with sex trafficking, gangs, or had pretty dangerous people in their lives. Anita had the tough task of keeping us safe. I really don't know how she did this for over fourteen years. She had been a single mom herself. Her kids are now in their thirties. She never had time to date or do much for herself except for an occasional pedicure. I'm sure I took her for granted at the time, but Anita is a total badass.

# XIX

# SPRING FORWARD

JUNE 14TH WAS bittersweet. Excitement filled the air since breakfast. Two of the girls in our house graduated. One of them was Mona. She was triumphant. Anita took the graduates out to get mani-pedis. I was happy for her and yet sad at what it meant for me. Mona was preparing to move out. I don't know how I would have made it through those difficult months without her. Although she was only eighteen, her wisdom and no-nonsense attitude cut through the massive wall around me. Her snarky sense of humor made me laugh again. Her compassion made me feel loved. She decided to go to school to become a social worker to help kids in foster care. I was not surprised. Her plan was to keep taking classes at the community college in the summer.

"There is no reason to wait until fall, I need to get this done," Mona said.

"I can't imagine coming home at the end of the day and seeing someone else sitting on your bed," I whined.

"Be nice," she said with a laugh. Then more seriously added, "It is your turn to help someone out of their sorrow."

I needed to be at Mona's graduation ceremony. Anita and her social worker were going, but none of her biological family would be there. When it was time to go, Mona came out of the bathroom with her hair in a sophisticated up-do. She was wearing a bold yellow dress, tall black boots, and bright red lipstick. I had never seen her wear makeup. Her happiness and pride radiated. I felt like maybe I should have put on something besides jeans, but it was too late to change. As we went into the auditorium, Mona rolled her separate way to join up with her class. Anita and I found seats as close to the front as possible because we wanted to get pictures. The room was decorated with flowers and streamers. The music was blasting, I could barely hear Anita when she tried to talk to me. I can only assume the students picked the music since it was hip-hop and rap. The ceremony was too long and my back hurt from sitting on the cold metal folding chairs. However, some of the speeches inspired me even as I resisted.

Finally, they called Mona's name. They had helped her get on stage before they began calling names from her class. This enabled her to seamlessly wheel herself into the lineup without any delay. When they called her name, her smile widened. As she raced over to accept her diploma, she did a 360-degree spin. The principal laughed and smiled warmly while handing Mona her diploma. They exchanged a few words, and Mona rolled to the other side of the stage to meet her group. It was at this point that I noticed tears were silently running down Anita's cheeks. We made eye contact.

"I am so proud of her. And I know you can do it too," Anita said.

Mona lived with Anita for almost two years. There was a lot between them that I could sense, even though I never saw them engage in deep conversations. Maybe that happened before I arrived? It seemed they had a deep understanding of each other.

After the ceremony, Mona wanted to go for a big seafood dinner. Many people on Mona's team had pitched in and given Anita money to make graduation day special. Lucky for me, Mona said it would be much more special if I were part of the celebration. Jennifer, the other girl who graduated, said she wanted to save her celebration for later. Jennifer was the fashionista at our house. She was a bit taller than me, and had straight long blonde hair that she straightened more before she'd go anywhere. She also put a lot of effort into doing her make-up. She wants to be a famous YouTuber and do makeup tutorials someday. She couldn't do it while in foster care because we aren't allowed to post public pictures or videos of ourselves online – "for our protection." Jennifer said she want-ed her graduation funds to purchase her new "I'm free wardrobe and some nice makeup." Her social worker also attended the graduation and said she'd give her a ride home. With that settled, Mona, Anita, and I headed to get some seafood.

The restaurant Mona chose was on the waterfront. We lucked out and there was one table left on the patio right on the water. I felt so fancy. The restaurant was crowded. I wondered how many of the people were tourists, or locals that got to eat like this on a regular basis, or maybe others were celebrating like we were?

"Order anything you want, we have plenty to cover it," Anita offered.

"Really, Anita? Anything."

"Yup. Honey, go for it. You deserve this. I'm so proud of you."

"Let's get the 'Seafeast'. It has Dungeness crab, snow crab, king crab, clams, mussels, shrimp, sausage, potatoes, and corn."

"Can we really?" I asked Anita.

"Absolutely." Anita beamed.

I was so excited I could barely keep myself in my chair. The last time I had a meal like that was on the coast with my mom and *papi* maybe six years ago. We chatted excitedly while we waited. The waiter came out with the huge met-al bowl containing all the delicious treats and dumped it in the middle of the table. We were each given a big wooden mallet, wooden boards to use as plates, and plastic bibs to wear.

"Have fun, ladies," he said.

And we did. None of us had anything this decadent in a long, long time. We smashed at the crab legs and shells flew into the air. We spent as much time laughing as we did eating.

When we got home, we were stuffed and tired. As usual, instead of sitting in the common room Mona and I went to ours. I told Mona I was happy for her and that she was an inspiration for me. Then, I started talking about how much I was going to miss her and how I didn't know what I would do without her.

She interrupted by snapping, "Hey today isn't about you! Let me just be happy."

We were silent for a long awkward moment after that, and then we started cracking up. When we finally stopped laughing, I mumbled under my breath.

"I love you, Mona."

"I love you too. We are sisters now."

She was the first friend, I ever told that I loved them. I guess maybe she was my first real friend after childhood. Even though Mona had been through hell, she had a huge heart and an enormous amount of love to give. Knowing her, changed me.

We spent the rest of the night talking about her next steps. She told me about how her Independent Living Program (ILP) helped her get a housing voucher and the basic necessities for her aPodment. Since Seattle is ridiculously expensive, she wasn't able to afford a real apartment. Her caseworkers had considered co-housing options for her, but they couldn't find any that were ADA accessible near her college.

"I prefer to live alone anyway. I don't want to be around drinking or drugs. And college students are kinda known for that. I need to stay focused. I've seen enough damage caused by booze and drugs already in my life. Don't worry, we'll still see each other. We will still be in the same town; I'm not going far."

"I hope so. I'm going to miss you so much."

"Hey, we know how to use the busses. We can get to each other anytime," she reminded me.

Over the next few weeks, I tried my best to be a supportive, helpful friend. Mona didn't have much to move out of Anita's. Since it was summer, I was only working on making up credits by completing 'credit retrieval' packets. During my free time, I took the bus to Mona's to help her set up her new home. She loved her classes and became part of a cool program that was set up for students who had been in foster care. It offered drop-in support, helped her pay for books and other supplies, helped with applying for financial aid, and even handed out free pizza for lunch on Friday.

"It's nice to meet other kid's that were in foster care when I go get pizza. Y'know like we never say, 'oh, you were in foster care too', but we all just know it. So, it's cool because we know that we understand what each other's lives were like."

"So, are there are lot of foster kids there?" I guess I thought Mona would be the only one for some reason. It gave me hope to know that other people that went through the system seemed to be doing ok.

"More than you'd think. Most Fridays there are at least five or ten. The director of the program is also great. She really takes the time to listen and is always there if we need a confidence boost, help understanding all the forms required by the school, or when we just want to vent," Mona said.

"She sounds awesome. I'm glad it's all going so great for you."

After I had "earned" my freedom and could travel by bus without a chaperone. I also met up with my mom covertly. I assume that everyone involved in my case knew that I would, but we still had our "supervised" visits at her social worker's office and no one asked if I was seeing my mom outside of the meetings. After mom OD'd, the hospital social worker convinced her to try going on methadone to help her completely off heroin and to prevent her from "jonesing." My mom was against taking drugs to get off drugs. Before she OD'd, she had been on the waiting list for months to get into an inpatient rehab where she could detox and get counseling. She had tried to get clean on the streets by herself. When she finally got so sick, she couldn't take it anymore; she decided to use just a little "to take the edge off."

That was when the OD'd happened. A lot of the smack on the street is laced with fentanyl, which can be deadly in even a small amount. The experience freaked her out, and she was ready to try anything to get off junk. That was when she decided methadone was the best option she had at the moment. At first, she went to get her dose every morning. Eventually, she would earn a prescription where she can have several doses at a time or "carries" as they call them at the clinic. While she was in the hospital, all her for abscesses were finally treated. It turns out she also had pneumonia, and that is why she was on oxygen when I visited her.

My mom wrestled a lot with her back pain since she stopped using. Opioids were the only kind of painkillers that worked to relieve the pain, but she knew it wasn't safe for her to take them anymore. Sleeping outside on the ground made her pain worse. At least in the summer, it wasn't cold and damp. Physically she was starting to look a little better, but she was still far too thin and looked older than her years. She always tried to remain upbeat when we saw each other, but she couldn't hide how broken her spirit was. Sometimes my *papi* still asked about her when he messaged me. They were each other's first loves.

I finally found the courage to tell him how she was actually doing. He was heartbroken. When they were together my mom barely even drank, she said she didn't like the way alcohol tasted and didn't understand why people drank stuff that made them feel sick after – especially since it tasted horrible. My *papi* tried to convince me he should try to come back so he could help us. I begged him not to. I was so afraid he'd die on the way up north and I would never see him again.

The housing crisis in Seattle was unbelievable, and the waiting lists were long. If you had children living with you, then you were considered a priority, but since I was already in foster care, my mom's application was being considered as a single woman. This was another flaw in the system that she kept trying to fight, but no one seemed to care or be able to figure out a way to help us be back together again. She hoped to at least get into one of the tiny house villages before the rain started again. She couldn't handle another winter outside, she said. As my mom talked about the fall, I realized she had lost hope that we would be back together by then. I felt guilty because, honestly, Anita's house was probably nicer than any place my mom would land after all she has been through. Apparently, the system was not designed to help people like us.

## XX

# AND IN A BLINK IT WAS FALL

SUMMER FLEW BY as usual. Before any of us felt ready, it was time to go back to school and the days became shorter and rainier. Within a week of Mona leaving, I had a new roommate. I asked Anita if she could wait a while for me to adjust. And once again, I was reminded this wasn't about me. Many teenage girls were waiting for more permanent placements because most foster parents don't like to take in teens. People want cute babies, not troubled youth. My new roommate, Tammi, has been in foster care on and off most of her life. Tammi is super tall and thin and loves to run. She may be the first person I ever met who actually likes to exercise. Tammi turned fifteen a few days before moving into our house. When she moved in, everyone in the house was called into the common room for a meeting. Anita tries hard to build community between us and it is always her hope that we will look out for each other. She felt it was essential for us to understand that Tammi had recently been diagnosed with epilepsy and what we should do if she had a seizure. Tammi wasn't part of the conversation. I found out later that Anita said she could tell us about the epilepsy or Tammi could talk to us herself. Tammi felt too uncomfortable and didn't want to do it, but understood why it was important that we all knew. Unlike with Mona, Tammi tended to hang out in the common room with the other girls and only came into our room when she was ready to sleep. This worked great for me, as I preferred to be alone now that Mona was gone.

Since I didn't have Mona to chat with in the evenings. I worked on the credit retrieval packets Francis kept giving me. I loved that I could do them at my own pace rather than having to wait for other people to finish their assignments before we could move on, or for the teacher to set the pace. SAC had periods of the day where you could drop in and get help from teachers of different subjects. You didn't even have to be in their class, they also helped those of us working on credit retrieval or doing self-paced courses. At first, I didn't go but then I finally (with many reminders from Francis) realized that if I went to the drop-in sessions, I didn't have to struggle with a type of math problem for hours, for example. The teacher could explain it and teach me how to do it. Then I could move on to the next thing.

During my time at SAC, I never met a teacher who was unwilling to repeat themselves or show us multiple ways to approach a problem. Every one of them seemed to actually want to teach us. Most of them had burnt out at traditional schools where the focus was on getting high test scores. Most of the teachers were also vocal about how much they disliked the way schools today treat students. SAC was supposed to be a school for us to go to until we caught up, but for many of us, it was a school where we felt safe, respected, and successful. We did not want to leave. Claudia, the principal, heard us when we told her that was how we felt. She said that the school would need to readjust, but she couldn't make kids that were enjoying her school leave. It was a big win for us.

With my sixteenth birthday right around the corner, I started incessantly asking Francis about how I could get a job.

"Have you started working with an Independent Living Program (ILP)?"

"Nope," I responded, "But Mona, my old roommate, said hers helped a lot."

"Let's have a meeting to think about your next steps. Do you mind if I invite your social worker and Anita?"

"I actually have no idea who my social worker is at the moment, but if you can figure that out, I'm ok with them coming to the meeting."

Sara, my favorite social worker, moved to Michigan to be closer to her family because she was having her first baby. Sara will be an awesome mom, I am sure. I'm happy for her but was so sad to hear she was leaving me, too.

A few days later, Francis passed me in the hall and asked me to come to chat with him when I had a moment. After I finished my history test, I asked for a pass to go see him. He told me he got in touch with Anita and my social worker. Anita said she could attend a meeting next Wednesday, but the social worker whose name I found out was Amy said she wouldn't be able to get to a meeting for at least a month or so. And generally, she only goes to the school if there "is some kind of problem." I told him I was not at all surprised. Francis said I should not worry, that he and Anita would help me get what I needed.

The next week, when we sat down together, we spent a bit of time talking about options for my ILP and what resources there were for me getting a job. Anita was worried that if I started working it would get in the way of my catching up with school. Francis reassured her that I was moving faster through the credit retrieval than most students and he felt good about my progress. We finally agreed that I would work no more than ten hours a week, for now. I immediately started doing the math. The minimum wage was $15 an hour, and I could work about forty hours a month, so that would be $600 a month. Anita would have to work with the social worker to get a bank account set up, and most of my earnings would have to go into an account that I didn't have complete access to until I was eighteen. I reminded them the plan was to use the money to get to México, so I didn't want to touch it until I was eighteen.

Next, we got to work trying to figure out who would hire me. I had zero skills.

Anita also said that she would make sure I got signed up for the ILP and she would keep on my new social worker until it happened. The people at the ILP could help me fill out job applications, learn how to manage my bank account, create a budget, and cook meals.

"So how do you feel about everything we talked about?" Francis asked at the end of our conversation.

"I feel like I'm going to be very busy," I replied.

I was ready, though. The busier I was, the faster time moved and the closer I felt to being free from the system. I still had days where I was depressed, frustrated, and felt hopeless but I didn't have time to let it drag me down.

"Promise me you will talk to me if it all feels like too much," Anita said warmly, she was such a mom. "I am here for you."

"Thanks, Anita. I know you are." I meant it too. Anita was a rock, how she handled all of us I will never know. But I am thankful for her.

At least once a month, Tina messaged me on Facebook. Her messages were short and usually just said something like, "I am thinking of you. Please call me." When my life became more routine, and I felt like I could actually hold it all together, I messaged her. I told her too much had happened to write it all in a message and asked if she wanted to meet for coffee somewhere. We met one day after school. It was fall, and there was a crispness in the air. Since it wasn't raining, we grabbed coffee to go and decided to take a walk. I told her everything that had gone on and about my mom OD'ing and how she was doing better with methadone.

"I still don't know why you left my house without telling me what was going on. And why you were afraid to message until now?" The way Tina spoke I could tell she felt hurt that I didn't confide in her. Tina had known me since I was little. She had always been like an aunt to me.

"Ok, here it goes. I didn't want you to think my mom was more of a fuck up than you already did. Or that I was a fuck up too. Tina, my mom and I talked about you – she feels like you gave up on her. Which I guess you kinda did. Would you please get in touch with her?"

"It was hard but.... you know what? You're right. She was my best friend. She needs me. I'm sorry, I wasn't there for both of you. I'll message her and see if she'll meet with me. Can you forgive me?"

"She's still her. She needs us all."

Tina seemed to have life figured out, but I guess she makes mistakes too. She had a great job, a nice car, and a beautiful home. Tina reassured me that her life wasn't that perfect, but from where I stood it looked great.

"How can I help? I love you and I want to do everything I can to help you reach your dreams."

I told her about my plan to go to México to be with my *papi*. She thought it was terrific: she'd been to México a few times on vacation, but only to the beach.

Tina agreed to go through the process with the state (background checks and everything), so that she could pick me up and take me out for day trips. For the rest of my time in care, Tina and I tried to have at least one special day a month. It was nice to have her to myself. I didn't have to share her attention with any of the girls in the group home. It was just Tina and I. Our mini-adventures always included food. Sometimes we went for walks in Discovery Park, took the ferry over to Bainbridge Island, or sat on the beach at Golden Gardens. When it was raining, we went bowling or to see a movie. The movies were never my first choice because I loved talking to her. She and my mom had started talking again too. We only broke the rule of bringing my mom along a couple of times; generally, it was to take her food. She had kept herself off dope, but she was still incredibly thin. When I hugged her, I felt like she would break.

When the rainy dark days came again, my mom was still on the waiting list for housing. I wanted so badly to ask Tina if my mom could live with her, but Tina was clear that she "had boundaries." I knew there was no guarantee at this point that my mom wouldn't start using again. She needed more time, more counseling, and more hope. I also didn't want to damage my relationship with Tina. I like the way things were between us. I had also wondered if I could have lived with her. She had a good job and everything, I am sure she would have passed the home study. I also stayed silent about that desire. I guess when you spend so much time fighting those systems you learn to pick your battles. I had yet another social worker; the one that couldn't find time to meet with Francis, Anita, and I didn't last two months. Even when I did try to advocate for myself, and they said yes, the social worker that said yes would be gone before anything could change.

# XXI

# SWEET 16

AT LAST, MY sixteenth birthday came. I was allowed to celebrate with Mona, Tina, and my mom. Once again, eating was the main event. Tina's treat. I choose Mexican food. I ate my favorite, seafood enchiladas. I felt terrible that they were so expensive, but Tina insisted we get anything we want. Mona admitted she was excited because as a "starving college student" she has been living on ramen, eggs, peanut butter and jelly, and an occasional Dick's hamburger (a Seattle classic). Mona told us about her classes and how much she enjoyed learning. I could tell my mom felt uncomfortable during the whole dinner. Everyone was sharing their successes and their plans for the future, and my mom was just trying to make it through the day. She laughed along with us, but it was out of duty, not joy. I wished some services or someone could help her. I shared that I had ten job applications filled out and that tomorrow I would start delivering them. I realized even talking about the job hunt only made my mom feel worse. She had applied for many positions, but with no permanent address or phone, it makes it nearly impossible to get hired. I quickly switched the subject. After dinner, Tina drove us all home. She dropped off Mona first and then me. I think she knew watching my mom walk back into the tent city would not be the best ending to my birthday celebration.

Over the next few weeks, I applied for about twenty jobs. Mostly at fast-food restaurants and grocery stores. Although the thought of working at a fast-food place wholly disgusted me, I kept focusing on my goal of earning money to get to my *papi*. I lucked out and got a job at Safeway. I would be trained to bag groceries and to stock shelves. It was also walking distance from Anita's house, so I didn't even have to take the bus. I was ecstatic. Once work started, I had to learn how to manage my time and keep track of everything I had to do. I missed a couple of homework assignments at school just because I completely forgot about them. I was busier than I had ever been in my life. The stakes were high, if work interfered with school I would have to quit. I went to Francis immediately when I saw my grades were dropping. I did not want to have to give up.

"How are you keeping track of what you need to get done? Francis asked.

"I just remember."

"Interesting. I thought you came to see me because you forgot some assignments?" He replied.

"Uh. Yeah. That. Guess, I don't remember everything," I admitted.

"Can I show you a couple apps I have on my phone to keep track of to-do items and larger projects?"

"Sure, I've never been so busy before. I guess I have to learn to manage it all."

Francis helped me understand that before I had a lot going on, I could remember everything I needed to do. Anita kept track of meetings with my social worker, doctor's appointments, and stuff like that. Keeping track of my own stuff was completely new.

"Everyone needs a way to track their to-do items. It isn't just you." Francis always had a way of making me feel like I wasn't a failure or the only one struggling.

That night, I looked at a bunch of apps and downloaded a few that I thought would help. The next day, I checked in with Francis and he helped me create a plan for tracking all my projects including my group activities with my ILP, job schedule (which changed weekly), and my homework.

I wouldn't say I was content during that time. My focus was always on turning eighteen and getting out of the system. However, my life was calmer than it had been in a very long time. I still wanted to be with my mom, and I worried about her health and safety constantly. Mona reminded me though that, in the long run, I could do much more for her if I had an education and some money. Mona was incredibly busy with school, but she always made time to talk with me. I feel like I will forever be in debt to her. Mona gave me hope during that excruciatingly difficult time in my life. She rarely seemed to be the one that needed to talk, vent, cry, or yell. Her resilience and tenacity still blow my mind. She even found energy to tutor international students who were struggling with the material because they were still learning English.

# XXII

# TIME MOVES ON

FOR THE FIRST time in as long as I could remember, my life became kind of boring and uneventful. I was ok with that. I found my groove and was able to work and go to school at the same time. During the summer, I worked as much as everyone would let me and I kept putting money away so that I could get to México. Everyone told me that I shouldn't even think about going and that it would never happen. If there was anyone around that knew me for a short time they'd jump in and say something like, "I can tell you don't know Didi, that girl is determined. She is going to make this happen."

When Francis and I sat down to plan out my junior year, I was surprised at how many credits I was able to make up.

"Didi, I have an idea I'd like to run by you."

"What's up?"

"I was thinking since you've been doing so great, you might want to start taking classes at the community college. You could earn your associate's degree and graduate at the same time."

"What? What are you saying? I could take classes with Mona?"

"Well, maybe not with Mona, she's a little ahead. Isn't she almost ready to graduate?"

"Yeah, sorry. I guess I was just excited. Tell me more about this? How can I pay for it?"

"It's actually free to students in our schools."

"Yes, yes, tell me how to do this."

"I wasn't sure how'd you feel about it. I'm glad you're excited I think this will be a great experience for you."

We got to work creating a plan and Francis helped me with all the paperwork. No one in my family has been to college. I got to start at sixteen and get my associates without paying for it, too. I didn't get to take any classes with Mona but we grabbed coffee between classes sometimes. It was nice to know she was there. She introduced me to the people at the program on campus for students who had been in foster care. Even though most of the other students were much older than I and already out of care, it was great connecting with them and it felt like I had older siblings who always had my back.

I tried to see my mom every couple of weeks, even though I was juggling school and work. She met a guy who seemed nice. He had an RV and invited her to stay with him, so she was off the streets during the winter. She was still taking methadone and said she was sometimes tempted but didn't do anything else. Yet she didn't have her vibrancy back and admitted dealing with her back pain was a constant struggle. In the spring, she finally got the energy to start fighting for disability payments. One of the hardest conversations I ever had was the day that I told her about my plans to go to México to be with my *papi*. All this time I kept it a secret from her because I couldn't stand the thought of hurting her.

"I thought we'd be together after you got out of the system." My mom sobbed.

"I know. I thought that, too. But I want to know him. I want to know where he has lived all these years. I'm also tired of how people treat me here because I'm Mexican. I want to be surrounded by people who look like me. I want to know my *tías*, *primos*, and my *abuelita*. I want to get better at Spanish. Mom, I love you and I need to do this."

We sat silently weeping. My mom leaned her head on my shoulder and slowly put her arms around me. Then, she kissed me on the check and looked straight into my eyes.

"Do it. I want you to experience the world and to know your *papi* again. He is a beautiful person. My first and only love. Please come back to see me though. Please."

"Of course! Thank you for understanding. I love you, *mamá*."

# XXIII

# SOUTH OF THE BORDER

Is this a dream? I pinch myself. I really did it. No one would believe me that, after I got out of foster care, I would be heading to México. Mona was right all along; I don't think I could have done this without her. It was tough to get my shit together, to focus, to save money, to get my passport. But I did it! As the plane got closer to Morelia, I knew I should try to sleep. I had been up all night, but my excitement kept me going.

As the wheels bounced on the runaway, my heart raced. We were on the ground. I was in México! I only had a backpack with me, so I didn't even have to wait for my bags. Security and immigration were a breeze compared to getting through TSA in the States. Everyone was so friendly. They asked me where I was going and what my purpose was in México.

"*Estoy visitando a mi papá,*" I beamed.

"*¿Dónde vive tu papá?*" They asked.

"Pátzcuaro," I answered.

They told me how beautiful it was there, and how they love to go the Cantoya Fest every year. That was it, all they said before handing me my tourist card.

"*¡Buen viaje!*" They said.

I almost ran to the information booth to ask where I could catch the bus to Pátzcuaro. I realized then that, even though I was in an airport, I was the only one rushing. I loved seeing the families greet each other with hugs and kisses. I couldn't wait to be surrounded by my family, too.

I'm so lucky that my *papi* taught me to read and speak Spanish. I can imagine immigration may have been harder if I only spoke English. I also had no problem asking about the buses. The lady at the information desk told me the next bus to Pátzcuaro would leave in two hours. I couldn't believe after years of waiting; I would be with my *papi* soon.

I went to the ATM to get some pesos and then looked for something to eat. I was so hungry. I couldn't wait to eat *tacos*, *churros*, and *chiles rellenos*, but I settled for a packaged sandwich and some chips. The airport was tiny and didn't have many choices. Then I went outside to wait. The sun was just coming up. It was so quiet.

I sat on a cement bench and tried to absorb every sight and sound. In the distance, I heard a rooster crowing and a cow mooing. For the first time in my life, everyone around me was brown. It felt a little weird to not be the only Mexican! I felt entirely anonymous and like sitting on that bench was exactly where I belonged. It wasn't until I got on the bus and we headed out that I realized the airport was out in the middle of nowhere. The hills lining the roadside were unbelievably green, and the clouds hung low to the ground. Just like my *papi* said, it reminded me of the Pacific Northwest. It was the rainy season, and everything smelled fresh and damp.

A momma and two little ones sat down next to me. She smiled warmly and asked if I was heading on a trip or coming back. I probably gave her too much information in a super short time because of my excitement. Let's just say within moments she knew all about my *papi* and why I was heading to Pátzcuaro.

As the bus approached Pátzcuaro, my heart started beating faster. I felt like I was in a dream state, maybe it was from the many flights and almost a full day of travel? Or because I had been dreaming of the moment for years. Everyone said it wasn't going to happen. How could a kid like me get it together to travel to a different country by myself? Where would I get the money? And then there is the danger. "México is so dangerous," they all said. As if Seattle isn't? As if people didn't get shot there all the time? "Watch out for the *narcos*," they said. Ha, right. As if Seattle doesn't have any drugs.

The *mamá* sitting next to me let me know when we had about twenty minutes until we got to Pátzcuaro. I messaged my *papi* and told him we were almost there. He responded immediately: "*no puedo esperar a verte, mija.*" Goosebumps covered my body. My seatmate asked if I was cold and wanted her to put the window up. I was a little embarrassed.

"*No, sólo estoy emocional y emocionada.*"

"*¡Pronto estarás con papá!*" She patted my leg gently and smiled warmly.

As we rode through the valley, I couldn't believe how many variations of green I saw. It was misty and thick clouds hung below the tops of the mountains. The mountains looked a lot like home, except they were missing the snow caps. I loved looking out the windows and seeing the cows and horses. The scenery was serene.

The bus came to a stop, I got excited but the driver was just paying a toll. We were off again in no time, though. I saw on the street sign that Pátzcuaro was only twelve kilometers away. I could barely stay seated. Soon buildings started lining both sides of the street, instead of hills. We were in town. I could smell roasting chicken. We passed a fruit stand overflowing with mangos, watermelons, papaya, jicama, and avocados. I couldn't wait to taste that fresh fruit.

Finally, the bus came to a stop again. There was a group of people that seemed like they were waiting for the bus. Off to the side, there was a man holding a bunch of flowers. He was wearing a straw hat and looking down so I couldn't see his face. I kept scanning the group as I grabbed my backpack and waited for the people in the front of the bus to exit. Then, the man looked up, and we made eye contact. It was my *papá*.

I had to hold back the temptation to push my way through the crowd to get off the bus. Patience isn't my strength. I switched from one foot to the other trying to dissipate my anxiousness as I waited for my turn to exit. As I walked down the stairs, I thought to myself "don't cry." Once my feet hit the ground, I ran to him. He wrapped his arms around me and said "*¡bienvenida a casa, mija!*" My heart was full, and the tears flowed from joy instead of sorrow.

※

# Acknowledgements

I am humbled and grateful to offer these words to my readers; this is a story I could not have written alone. If my foster daughter hadn't moved into my home and heart nearly 17 years ago, my career would have been radically different, and this book would not exist. She inspired me to learn how to be a better advocate for youth in care. I am also immensely grateful to all my previous clients and research participants who trusted me and shared their life histories. They taught me more about the world than any class ever could. This book is part of the promise I made to them – that I would share their stories to help others. To Drs. Deanne Unruh and Lauren Lindstrom who would not let me quit my doctoral program (even when I wanted to) and believed my dissertation research about youth who experienced foster care was important. Thanks to Ariel Gore and Nina Packenbush, who guided me through my writing process with their fantastic courses, and to the Wayward Writers whose feedback helped me create richer characters and a more compelling story. To my student, Carlos Reyes, who generously offered to read my novel and provide feedback over his spring break. Tremendous gratitude for León Herrera, my publisher, who read every word, verified my Spanish translations, and believed Didi's story should be out in the world. Of course, I would be remiss if I did not thank my bio and found family for their unconditional support and love. You are my world: Marcia Griffith, Marciana Romero, Alesandro Harwick, Brittaney Drake, and Jessica Mendoza. And finally, to Mexico, thank you for your graciousness, giving me time and space to write, and making us feel like we are home.

# About the author

Robin Harwick, Ph.D., is a mother, author, educator, and consultant. She has spent years coaching youth and young adults on how to achieve their dreams. After an unexpected layoff, in 2017, she decided it was time to "walk her talk." She pulled her teenage son from school, loaded up their van with their two dogs, and left Seattle for Mexico! What was supposed to be a short visit with family ended in putting down roots and making Mexico their home.

Dr. Harwick is dedicated to improving children and families' lives through research, teaching, and service. She has been a member of research teams since 1995. Robin also worked extensively in the direct service of children and families as a parent educator, home visitor, and therapeutic foster parent. Much of Dr. Harwick's work focuses on the transition to adulthood, child welfare, and substance use disorders. Additionally, she is the founder and director of The Pearl Remote Democratic High School. Her school is a home-school partnership that offers teens an empowering educational experience from anywhere in the world.

In collaboration with Dr. Kimberly Douglass, Robin co-authored "You Are the Revolution: Education that Empowers your Black Child and Strengthens your Family." She is also published in numerous peer-reviewed journals, blogs, zines, and anthologies.

robinharwick.com

Printed in Great Britain
by Amazon